Clara Kern Bayliss
Philippine Folk Tales

Clara Kern Bayliss
Philippine Folk Tales

Philippine Folk Tales

By Clara Kern Bayliss

CONTENTS

Part	I	1
Part	II	9
Part	III	41
Part	IV	59
Part	V	61
Part	VI	63

PART 1

Philippine Folk Takes

The Monkey and the Turtle.

One day a Monkey met a Turtle on the road, and asked, "Where are you going?"

"I am going to find something to eat, for I have had no food for three whole days," said the Turtle.

"I too am hungry," said the Monkey; "and since we are both hungry, let us go together and hunt food for our stomachs' sake."

They soon became good friends and chatted along the way, so that the time passed quickly. Before they had gone far, the Monkey saw a large bunch of yellow bananas on a tree at a distance.

"Oh, what a good sight that is!" cried he. "Don't you see the bananas hanging on that banana-tree? . They are fine! I can taste them already."

But the Turtle was short-sighted and could not see them. By and by they came near the tree, and then he saw them. The two friends were very glad. The mere sight of the ripe, yellow fruit seemed to assuage their hunger.

But the Turtle could not climb the tree, so he agreed that the Monkey should go up alone and should throw some of the fruit down to him. The Monkey was up in a flash; and, seating himself comfortably, he began to eat the finest of the fruit, and forgot to drop any down to the Turtle waiting below. The Turtle called for some, but the Monkey pretended not to hear. He ate even the peelings, and refused to drop a bit to his friend, who was patiently begging under the tree.

At last the Turtle became angry, very angry indeed: "so he thought he would revenge" (as my informant puts it). While the Monkey was having a good time, and filling his stomach, the Turtle gathered sharp, broken pieces of glass, and stuck them, one by one, all around the banana-tree. Then he hid himself under a cocoanut-shell not far away. This shell had a hole in the top to allow the air to enter. That was why the Turtle chose it for his hiding-place.

The Monkey could not eat all the bananas, for there were enough to last a good-sized family several days; "but he ate all what he can," and by and by came down the tree with great difficulty, for the glass was so sharp that it cut even the tough hand of the Monkey. He had a hard time, and his hands were cut in many places. The Turtle thought he had his revenge, and was not so angry as before.

But the Monkey was now very angry at the trick that had been played upon him, and began looking for the Turtle, intending to kill him. For some time he could not find his foe, and, being very tired, he sat down on the cocoanut-shell near by. His weariness increased his anger at the Turtle very much.

He sat on the shell for a long time, suffering from his wounds, and wondering where to find the Turtle,—his former friend, but now his enemy. Because of the disturbance of the shell, the Turtle inside could not help making a noise. This the Monkey heard; and he was surprised, for he could not determine whence the sound came. At last he lifted his stool, and there found his foe the Turtle.

"Ha! Here you are!" he cried. "Pray now, for it is the end of your life."

He picked up the Turtle by the neck and carried him near the riverbank, where he meant to kill him. He took a mortar and pestle, and built a big fire, intending to pound him to powder or burn him to death. When everything was ready, he told the Turtle to choose whether he should die in the fire or be "grounded" in the mortar. The Turtle begged for his life; but when he found it was in vain, he prayed to be thrown into the fire or ground in the mortar,—anything except be thrown into the water. On hearing this, the Monkey picked the Turtle up in his bleeding fingers, and with all his might threw him into the middle of the stream.

Then the Turtle was very glad. He chuckled at his own wit, and laughed at the foolishness of the Monkey. He came up to the surface of the water and mocked at the Monkey, saying, "This is my home. The water is my home."

This made the Monkey so angry that he lost his self-possession entirely. He jumped into the middle of the river after the Turtle, and was drowned.

Since that day monkeys and turtles have been bitter enemies.

How the Farmer Deceived the Demon.

Very many years ago, in a far-away land where the trees never changed their green leaves and where the birds always sang, there lived on an island a farmer with a large family. Though all alone on the island and knowing nothing of people in the outer world, they were always happy,—as happy as the laughing rills that rippled past their home. They had no great wealth, depending from year to year on the crops which the father raised. They needed no money, for they lacked nothing; and they never sold their produce, for no people were near to buy.

One day in the middle of the year, after the crops were well started, a loud, unusual roar was heard. Suddenly a stiff gale blew up from the southwest, and with it came clouds which quickly hid the entire sky. The day turned to night. The birds ceased to sing and went to their nests. The wild beasts ran to their caves. The family sought shelter in the house from a heavy downpour of rain which continued for many days and nights. So long did it last that they became very anxious about the condition of things around them.

On the eighth day the birds again began to sing, and the sun was, as usual, bright. The farmer arose early and went out to look at his fields, but, lo! his crop was all destroyed. He went back to the house and told the family that the water-god was angry and had washed away all that he had hoped to have for the coming year.

What were they to do? The supply in the house was getting low and it was too late to raise another crop. The father worried night and day, for he did not know how he could keep his children from starvation.

One day he made a long journey and came into a place that was strange to him. He had never before seen the like of it. But in the midst of a broad meadow he saw a tree with spreading branches like an elm, and as his legs and back were stiff from walking, he went over and sat down under it. Presently, looking up, he discovered that on the tree were large red fruits. He climbed up and brought some down, and after satisfying his hunger he fell asleep.

He had not slept long when he was awakened by a loud noise. The owner of the place was coming. He was fearful to look upon. His body was like that of a person, but he was of enormous size; and he had a long tail, and two horns growing out of his head. The farmer was frightened and did not know what to do. He stood motionless till the master came up and began to talk to him. Then he explained that he had come there in search of food to keep his family alive. The monster was delighted to hear this, for he saw that he had the man and the man's family in his power. He told the traveller that in return for a certain promise he would help him out of his troubles.

The demon, as he was called by some travellers to that land, showed the farmer a smooth, round stone, which, he said, gave its possessor the power of a magician. He offered to lend this to the farmer for five years, if at the expiration of that time the farmer and family would become his slaves. The farmer consented.

Then the demon was glad. He said to the farmer, "You must squeeze the stone when you wish to become invisible; and must put it in your mouth when you wish to return to human form."

The man tried the power of the magic stone. He squeezed it, and instantly became invisible to the demon; but he bade him farewell, and promised to meet him in the same place at the appointed time.

In this invisible form the man crossed the water that washed the shore of the island on which he lived. There he found a people who lived in communities. He wanted something to eat, so he went into the shops; but he found that a restaurant owned by a Chinaman was the one to which most people of the city went. He put the stone in his mouth, thus appearing in visible form, and, entering the restaurant, ordered the best food he could find. He finished his meal quickly and went out. The waiter, perceiving that he did not pay, followed him. The man had no money; so he squeezed the stone and shot up into the air without being seen. The Chinaman, alarmed by the cry of the waiter, came out and ran in all directions, trying to find and catch the man. No one could find him; and the people thought he must indeed be a fast runner to escape so quickly, for they did not know of the gift of the demon.

Not far from that place he saw groups of men and women going in and out of a large building. It was a bank. The farmer went in to see what he could find. There he saw bags of money, gold and silver. He chuckled with joy at this opportunity. In order to use his hands freely, he put the stone in his mouth; but before he could fill all his pockets with money, he was discovered by the two guards, who began to pound him on the head. He struggled to save his life, and finally took the stone out of his mouth and squeezed it. Instantly he vanished from their sight; but he was vexed at the beating he had received, so he carried off all the gold they had in the bank. The people inside as well as outside the building became crazy. They ran about in all directions, not knowing why. Some called the firemen, thinking the bank was on fire; but nothing had happened, except that the farmer was gone and the two guards were "half dead frightened." They danced up and down the streets in great excitement, but could not utter a word.

Straight home went the farmer, not stopping by the way. His wife and children were awaiting him. He gave them the money, and told them all about the fortune which he had gotten from the man on their own island,—told all his secrets. Prosperous they became, and with the money which he had brought they purchased all they needed from the city just opposite them.

The time passed so pleasantly that the man was surprised to discover that his promise would be due in two more days. He made preparations to go back to the land of his master. Arrived there, he met the same monster under the same tree. The demon was displeased to see the old man alone, without the family which also had been promised. He told the man that he would shut him in a cave and then would go and capture those left at home.

But the farmer would not go to the cave. The demon tried to pull him into a deep hole. Both struggled; and at last the farmer squeezed the magic stone and disappeared. He took a green branch of the tree and beat the demon. The demon surrendered. He begged for mercy.

The farmer went home, and from that day thought no more of the demon. He knew that while he held the stone the monster would never come to trouble him. And the family lived on in peace and happiness, as they had done before the water-god became angry with them.

Benito, the Faithful Servant.

On a time there lived in a village a poor man and his wife, who had a son named Benito. The one ambition of the lad from his earliest youth was that he might be a help to the family in their struggle for a living.

But the years went by, and he saw no opportunity until one day, as they sat at dinner, his father fell to talking about the young King who lived at a distance from the village, in a beautiful palace kept by a retinue of servants. The boy was glad to hear this, and asked his parents to let him become one of the servants of this great ruler. The mother protested, fearing that her son could not please his Royal Majesty; but the boy was so eager to try his fortune that at last he was permitted to do so.

The next day his mother prepared food for him to eat on the journey, and be started for the palace. The journey was tiresome; and when he reached the palace he had difficulty in obtaining an audience with the King. But when he succeeded and made known his wish, the monarch detected a charming personality hidden within the ragged clothes, and, believing the lad would make a willing servant, he accepted him.

The servants of his Majesty had many duties. Theirs was not a life of ease, but of hard work. The very next day the King called Benito, and said, "I want you to bring me a certain beautiful princess who lives in a land across the sea; and if you fail to do it, you will be punished."

Benito did not know how he was to do it; but he asked no questions, and unhesitatingly answered, "I will, my lord."

That same day he provided himself with everything he needed for the journey and set off. He travelled a long distance until he came to the heart of a thick forest, where he saw a large bird which said to him, "Oh, my friend! please take away these strings that are wrapped all about me. If you will, I will help you whenever you call upon me."

Benito released the bird and asked it its name. It replied, "Sparrow-hawk," and flew away. Benito continued his journey until he came to the seashore. There he could see no way of getting across, and, remembering what the King had said if he failed, he stood looking out over the sea, feeling very sad. The huge King of the Fishes saw him, and swam toward him. "Why are you so sad?" asked the Fish.

"I wish to cross the sea to find the beautiful Princess," replied the youth.

"Get on my back and I will take you across," said the King of the

Fishes.

Benito rode on the back of the Fish and crossed the sea. As soon as he reached the other side, a fairy in the form of a woman appeared to him, and became a great aid to him in his adventure. She knew exactly what he wanted; so she told him that the Princess was shut up in a castle guarded by giants, and that he would have to fight the giants before he could reach her. For this purpose she gave him a magic sword, which would kill on the instant anything it touched.

Benito now felt sure he could take the Princess from her cruel guardsmen. He went to the castle, and there he saw many giants round about it. When the giants saw him coming, they went out to meet him, thinking to take him captive. They were so sure that they could easily do it, that they went forth unarmed. As they came near, he touched the foremost ones with his sword, and one after another they fell down dead. The other giants, seeing so many of their number slain, became terrified, and fled, leaving the castle unguarded.

The young man went to the Princess and told her that his master had sent him to bring her to his palace. The young Princess was only too glad to leave the land of the giants, where she had been held captive. So the two set out together for the King's palace.

When they came to the sea they rode across it on the back of the same fish that had carried Benito. They went through the forest, and at last came to the palace. Here they were received with the greatest rejoicings.

After a short time the King asked the Princess to become his wife. "I will, O King!" she replied, "if you will get the ring I lost in the sea as I was crossing it."

The monarch called Benito, and ordered him to find the ring which had been lost on their journey from the land of the giants.

Obedient to his master, Benito started, and travelled on and on till he came to the shore of the sea. There he stood, gazing sadly out over the waters, not knowing how he was to search for what lay at the bottom of the deep ocean.

Again the King of the Fishes came to him, asking the cause of his sadness. Benito replied, "The Princess lost her ring while we were crossing the sea, and I have been sent to find it."

The King-Fish summoned all the fishes to come to him. When they had assembled, he noticed that one was missing. He commanded the others to search for this one, and bring it to him. They found it under a stone, and it said, "I am so full! I have eaten so much that I cannot swim." So the larger ones took it by the tail and dragged it to their King.

"Why did you not come when summoned?" asked the King-Fish. "I was so full I could not swim," replied the Fish.

The King-Fish, suspecting that it had swallowed the ring, ordered it to be cut in two. The others cut it open, and, behold I there was the lost ornament. Benito thanked the King of the Fishes, took the ring, and brought it to the monarch.

When the great ruler got the ring, he said to the Princess, "Now that

I have your ring, will you become my wife?"

"I will be your wife," replied the Princess, "if you will find the earring I lost in the forest as I was journeying with Benito."

Instantly Benito was called, and was ordered to find the lost jewel. He was very weary from his former journey; but, mindful of his duty, he started for the forest, reaching it before the day was over. He searched for the earring faithfully, following the road which he and the Princess had taken; but all in vain. He was much discouraged, and sat down under a tree to rest. To his surprise a mouse of monstrous size appeared before him. It was the King of the Mice.

"Why are you so sad?" asked the Mouse.

"I am searching for an earring which the Princess lost as we passed through the forest, but am unable to find it."

"I will find it for you," said the King-Mouse.

Benito's face brightened at hearing this. The King-Mouse called all his followers, and all but one little mouse responded. Then the King of the Mice ordered some of his subjects to find the absent one. They found him in a small hole among the bamboo-trees. He said he could not go because he was so satisfied (sated). So the others pulled him along to their master; and he, finding that there was something hard within the little mouse, ordered him to be cut open. It was done; and there was the very earring for which the tired servant was looking. Benito took it, thanked the King of the Mice, and brought the earring to his own King.

When the monarch received it, he immediately restored it to its owner and asked, "Will you now become my wife?"

"Oh, dear King!" responded the Princess, "I have only one more thing to ask of you; and if you will grant it, I will be your wife forever."

The King, pleased with his former successes, said, "Tell me what it is, and it shall be granted."

"If you will get some water from heaven," said the Princess, "and some water from the nether-world, I will become your wife. That is my last wish."

The King called Benito, and commanded him to get water from these two places. "I will, my King," said Benito; and he took some provisions and started. He came to the forest; but there he became confused, for he did not know in which direction to go to reach either of the places. Suddenly he recalled the promise of the bird he had helped the first time he entered the wood. He called the bird, and it soon appeared. He told it what he wanted, and it said, "I will get it for you."

He made two cups of bamboo, and tied one to each of the bird's legs. They were very light, and did not hinder the bearer at all. Away the bird flew, going very fast. Before the day was ended, it came back with each cup full of water, and told Benito that the one tied to its right leg contained water from heaven, and the one tied to its left leg contained water from the nether-world.

Benito untied the cups, taking great care of them. He was about to leave, when the bird asked him to tarry long enough to bury it, as the places to which it had been were so far away that it was weary unto death.

Benito did not like to bury the bird, but he soon saw that it really was dying, so he waited; and when it was dead, he buried it, feeling very sorry over the loss of so helpful a friend.

He went back to the palace and delivered the two kinds of water to his master. The Princess then asked the King to cut her in two and pour the water from heaven upon her. The King was not willing to do it, so she did it herself, asking the King to pour the water. This he did, and, lo! the Princess turned into the most beautiful woman that ever the sun shone on.

Then the King was desirous of becoming handsome; so he asked the Princess to pour the other cup of water over him after he cut himself. He cut himself, and she poured over his body the water from the nether-world; but from him there arose a spirit more ugly and ill-favored than imagination could picture. Fortunately, it soon vanished from sight.

The Princess then turned to Benito, and said, "You have been faithful in your duties to your master, kind to me in restoring the jewels I lost, and brave in delivering me from the cruel giants. You are the man I choose for my husband."

Benito could not refuse so lovely a lady. They were married amid great festivities, and became the king and queen of that broad and fertile land.

Benito gave his parents one of the finest portions of his kingdom, and furnished them with everything they could desire. From that time on they were all very happy,—so happy that the story of their bliss has come down through the centuries to us.

PART II

Visayan Folk-Tales.

Introduction.

These stories are intended to bring before the American public a few of the tales related by Visayan parents to their children, or by the public story-teller in the market, as the people gather to buy the material for the evening meal. It was only toward the close of a three years' stay in the Islands, in one province, and in neighboring places, and after a fair acquaintance with Spanish and a little knowledge of the native dialect had enabled us to obtain a closer insight into the home life of our pupils than would otherwise have been possible, that we ventured upon the collection of these tales, hoping that they might prove of interest to people at home. Many of the stories were written by our boys and girls as part of their work in English composition. Others were prepared by the native teachers, some of whom had been well educated by the Spaniards and had already learned to write very fair English. Indeed, a few were able, at about the time that these stories were written, to pass the civil service examination for appointment as insular teachers. The articles on the superstitious beliefs of the people were prepared by one of these teachers, so that they might be as nearly correct as possible.

As might be expected, the stories are often very crude and simple, presenting no difficult situations nor intricate plots. Sometimes they resemble well-known tales from other lands, although great care has been taken to collect only those from original sources.

The tales here presented were collected during the spring of 1904, in the island of Panay, belonging to the Visayan group of the Philippine Islands, and were obtained in our own class rooms, from native teachers and pupils. Mr. Maxfield was stationed at Iloilo, and Mr. Millington at Mandurriao, places five miles apart. We daily came in contact with about one thousand pupils. The tales were gathered in both places, and were found to be substantially alike, the differences being only in petty details. After collecting one version, we endeavored to ascertain whether the same narrative was current among natives in other localities of the island. We were surprised to discover that they seemed to be known wherever we became acquainted with the people and had obtained their confidence sufficiently to induce them to talk freely. There were often variations, but the framework was always the same. If any stories were obtained from native teachers who knew Spanish, we have always verified them by getting children or natives from other places, who knew no Spanish, to relate them, in order to assure ourselves that the narrative could not be a mere translation of a Spanish tale.

We who have collected these stories can claim little credit for any more than the mere arrangement of them, as, so far as possible, even the wording of the original manuscripts has been retained. Doubtless, much of the interest we have felt in the work is due to our personal acquaintance with the writers who put on paper for us these simple tales, yet we hope that they will not be wholly unattractive to those for whose sake they have been collected.

February, 1906.

B. L. M.

W. H. M.

How Jackyo Became Rich.

A long time ago there was a young man whose name was Jackyo. He was very poor, and by his daily labor could earn barely enough for his food and nothing at all for his clothes. He had a little farm at some distance from the village in which he lived, and on it raised a few poor crops.

One pleasant afternoon Jackyo started off to visit his farm. It was late when he reached it, and after he had finished inspecting his crops, he turned back homewards. But the bright day had gone and the sun had set. Night came on quickly, and the way was dark and lonely.

At last he could no longer see the road. Not a star was to be seen, and the only sounds he heard were the sad twitterings of the birds and soft rustling of the leaves as they were moved by the wind.

At last he entered a thick forest where the trees were very big. "What if I should meet some wild beast," thought Jackyo; but he added half aloud, "I must learn to be brave and face every danger."

It was not long before he was very sure that he could hear a deep roar. His heart beat fast, but he walked steadily forward, and soon the roar was repeated, this time nearer and more distinctly, and he saw in the dim light a great wild ox coming towards him.

He found a large hole in the trunk of a huge tree. "I will pass the night here in this tree," he said to himself.

In a little while an old man appeared. His body was covered with coarse hair and he was very ugly. He looked fiercely at Jackyo from head to foot and said: "What are you thinking of to come in here? Do you not know that this is the royal castle of the king of evil spirits?"

Jackyo became more frightened than before and for a long time he could not speak, but at last he stammered: "Excuse me, sir, but I cannot go home on account of the dark night. I pray you to let me rest here for a short time."

"I cannot let you stay here, because our king is not willing to help any one who does not belong to his kingdom. If he did so, his kingdom would be lost. But what is your name? Do you know how to sing?" said the old man.

"My name is Jackyo, and I know a little bit about singing," replied

Jackyo.

"Well," said the old man, "if you know any song, sing for me." Now Jackyo knew but one song, and that was about the names of the days of the week except Sunday. He did not like to sing it, but the old man urged him, saying: "If you do not sing, I will cut your head off." So Jackyo began to sing.

It happened that the king of the evil spirits, whose name was Mensaya, heard Jackyo's song and was very much interested in it. He called a servant, named Macquil, and said: "Macquil, go downstairs and see who is singing down there, and when you find him, bring him to me."

Jackyo went before the king, bowed to the floor, touching the carpet with his forehead, and stood humbly before the king.

"Let me hear your song," said the king. So Jackyo, with great respect, sang the only song he knew. Here it is:

Mon-day, Tues-day, Wednesday, Thurs-day, Fri-day, Sat-ur-day.

While he was singing, all the evil spirits in the cave gathered around him to hear his song, and Mensaya asked him to sing it over and over again. They were all so pleased with it that Mensaya ordered Macquil to give Jackyo a large quantity of gold and silver as a reward for his beautiful song.

When the morning came Jackyo returned home, full of joy, and became known as the richest man in the village.

Truth and Falsehood.

One day Truth started for the city to find some work. On his way he overtook Falsehood, who was going to the city for the same purpose. Falsehood asked permission to ride on the horse with Truth, and his request was granted.

On the way they questioned each other as to the sort of work they wanted. Truth stated that he intended to be a secretary, so that he might always be clean and white. Falsehood declared that he would be a cook, because then he would always have plenty of fine things to eat.

As they were riding along, they met a man carrying a corpse to the cemetery. He had no one to help him, and Truth, in his great pity for the man, jumped off his horse and helped him. After the corpse was buried, Truth asked: "Did you pray for the repose of the soul of the dead?" "No," was the reply, "I do not know how to pray, and I have no money to pay the priest for candles." Then Truth gave the man all the money he had, that he might have prayers said for the dead man, and went back to his companion.

When dinner time came, Falsehood was very angry at finding out that Truth had given all his money away, but finally proposed that they should go to the river and catch some fish for dinner. When they arrived at the river, they found some fish which had been caught in a shallow pool near the bank, and caught all they wanted. But Truth was very sorry for the fish, and threw his half back into the river. Falsehood murmured at him and said: "It would have been better for you to give them to me. If I had known that you would throw them into the river, I would not have given you any of them." Then they rode on. As they were going through a thick wood in the heart of the mountain they heard a noise as of crying, far away. Truth went forward to find what it was, but Falsehood, trembling with fear, hid himself close behind his comrade. At last they saw seven little eagles in a nest high in a tree. They were crying with hunger, and their mother was nowhere to be seen. Truth was sorry for them, and killed his horse, giving some of the meat to the young eagles, and spreading the rest on the ground beneath the tree, so that the mother-bird might find it.

Falsehood hated his comrade for having killed the horse, because now they were obliged to travel on foot. They went down the mountain, and entering the city, presented themselves before the king, desiring to be taken into his service, the one as secretary and the other as cook. The king granted both requests.

When Falsehood saw that his former companion sat at the table with the king and was always clean and dressed in good clothes, while he himself was dirty and had to eat in the kitchen, he was very angry and determined to do something to ruin the one whom now he hated so bitterly.

One day the king and queen went to sail on the sea. As they were far from land, the queen dropped her ring overboard. When Falsehood heard of the accident, he went to the king and said: "My Lord, the King, my friend—your secretary—has told me that he was endowed with magic powers and is able to find the queen's ring. He says if he does not find it he is willing for you to hang him."

The king immediately sent for Truth, and said to him: "Find the queen's ring without delay, or I will have you hanged early to-morrow morning."

Truth went down to the shore, but seeing how impossible it would be to find the ring, began to weep. A fish came near, and floating on top of the water, asked, "Why are you weeping?"

"I weep," Truth replied, "because the king will hang me early to-morrow morning unless I find the queen's ring, which has fallen into the sea."

The fish swam out and got the ring and gave it to Truth. Then he said:

"I am one of the fishes which you found on the bank of the river and

threw back into the water. As you helped me when I was in trouble,

I am very glad that I have been able to help you now."

On another day, Falsehood went to the king and said: "My Lord King, do you remember what I told you the other day?"

"Yes," replied the king, "and I believe you told me the truth, as the ring has been found."

"Well," replied Falsehood, "my friend told me last night that he is a great magician and that he is willing for you to hang him in the sight of all the people, since it will not hurt him."

The king sent for Truth and told him: "I know what you have said to your friend. To-morrow I will have you hanged in the sight of all the people, and we will see whether you are the great magician you claim to be."

That night Truth could not sleep. About midnight, as he was in great distress, a spirit suddenly appeared to him and asked what was the cause of his grief. Truth related his trouble, and the spirit said: "Do not weep. To-morrow morning I will take your form and wear your clothes, and let them hang me."

The next morning, just at dawn, the spirit put on Truth's clothes and went out to be hanged. Many people came to see the hanging, and after it was over, returned to their homes. What was the astonishment of the king and those with him when, upon their return to the palace, they found Truth there before them, alive and well!

That night the spirit appeared to Truth and said: "I am the spirit of the dead man for whom you gave your money that prayers might be said for the repose of his soul." Then it disappeared.

On another day Falsehood appeared before the king and said: "My Lord the King, my friend the secretary told me last night that if you would let him marry your daughter, in one night his wife should bring forth three children." The king sent for Truth and said: "I will give you my daughter to be your wife and if to-night she does not bear three children, I will have you buried alive to-morrow morning."

So they were married. But at midnight, as Truth lay awake thinking of the fate that was in store for him in the morning, an eagle flew through the window, and asked the cause of his sorrow. Truth related his tale, and the eagle said: "Do not worry; I will take care of that." Then he flew away, but just before the break of day three eagles came, each bearing a new-born babe. Truth awakened the princess and said to her: "My dear wife, these are our children. We must love them and take good care of them."

Then the king, who had been awakened by the noise of children crying, sent to ask what it was all about. When he heard the news he came into the tower where the princess was, and when he saw the children he was overcome with joy; for he had no sons, and greatly desired to have an heir to his throne. So the king made a great feast and gave over his crown and sceptre to his son-in-law, to be king in his stead.

Thus we see that those who help others when in trouble shall themselves be aided when they are in difficulty.

Camanla and Parotpot.

Camanla was a very poor but very busy man, and always praising his own work. When he talked with other people he ended every third or fourth word with "la," which was the last syllable of his name and is a word of praise.

One day he made a boat, and when it was finished he began to talk to it. These were his words: "My boat, la, you may go, la, to find a pretty lady, la, for my wife, la, to make me happy, la." Then his boat started to sail without anybody to manage it. When she reached a large town she stopped in the river, near where the pretty daughters of some rich men of the town were taking a walk. They were accustomed to take any boat they might find and use it when they wished to cross the river, returning in the same way.

As Camanla's boat was there and looked very fine, the young ladies decided to cross the river in it. The youngest was the first to jump into the boat. When the little boat felt that some one had come on board, she ran away, carrying the lady.

When Camanla saw his boat coming, he began to praise it, saying: "My boat, la, is coming, la, to bring me, la, my pretty lady, to marry me, la." Very soon the boat anchored, and he went down to receive the lady, whom he soon married. Then was Camanla happy, but one day he had no food to give his wife, so he made a little taon, or fish trap, and said to it: "My pretty taon, la, you may go, la, to the river, la, to get me some fish, la." The taon then walked toward the river, and soon came back, full of fish. Camanla was an object of envy to all the world.

His happiness was soon heard of by his friend Parotpot, who became very envious. At last he went to Camanla's house. When he met his friend, he said to him: "You are very happy, my friend, and I envy you." Camanla replied: "Yes, I am very fortunate. I have my little boat that sails every day to get my food, and a little taon that goes to the river and brings me fine fish."

Parotpot returned sadly home. He concluded to build a boat like his friend's, but Parotpot, when he talked, ended every third or fourth word with "pot," (pronounced po) the ending of his name: This word has a scornful meaning. When the boat was finished, he began to talk to it as follows: "My boat, pot, you may go, pot, to find me a wife, pot, prettier than my friend's wife, pot." The boat sailed away, and reached a large river, just as some men were looking for a boat to take across the body of their grandmother, in order to bury it in the cemetery of the town. When they saw the boat they were glad to get across the river so easily, so they lifted the body and placed it in the boat. When the boat felt that something was on board, she sailed swiftly towards home, leaving the men behind. Parotpot was watching, and when he saw the boat coming, he began to talk thus: "My boat, pot, is coming, pot, to bring me, pot, a pretty lady, pot, to marry me, pot." But, alas! a dead grandmother, instead of a pretty lady! He was so angry that he seized his bolo and chopped the boat to pieces, leaving the body to float away.

But Parotpot thought that he might succeed better with a fish-trap, like his friend Camanla's. When he had finished it, he sent it to the river, saying: "My taon, pot, go now to the river, pot, and catch many fishes, pot, for my dinner, pot." The taon went. It was Sunday and the people of the town were killing cattle for their Sunday dinner, and throwing the waste into the river. All this filth floated into the taon and filled it. Then it ran back home. While the taon had been gone, Parotpot had been making preparations for a great dinner. He cooked the rice and washed the dishes, and then invited his friends to come to his house and share his excellent dinner. When he saw the taon coming, he said: "My taon, pot, is coming now, pot, to bring me many fine fish, pot, for my dinner, pot." When his neighbors saw what was in the taon, they laughed, and Parotpot said: "I can never be as happy as my friend Camanla." Then he took the taon and threw it into the fire.

Juan, the Student.

There was once a poor couple who lived happily in a quiet place. They had one son, named Juan, whom at first they loved very much; but afterwards, either because their extreme poverty made it difficult for them to support him, or because of his wickedness and waywardness, they began to hate him, and made plans to kill him.

In order to carry out this purpose, the father called his son to him one evening, and said: "My son, to-morrow we will go to the mountain to get some lumber with which to repair our house. I want you to prepare our breakfast very early, so that we may set out before the sun rises."

On the next morning they arose very early and ate their breakfast. As it consisted only of rice and a few small fishes, it was soon finished, and they set out for the mountain. When they had arrived at a lonely spot, the man seized his son and fastened him to a large tree. Then he took his bolo and cut down the tree in such a way as to cause it to fall on the boy and kill him. Then he returned home, thinking that he should have no more trouble on account of his son.

Early the next morning, the man heard a noise as of some one approaching the house. On opening a window he perceived his son, whom he supposed he had killed on the previous day, coming towards the house and bearing a heavy load of wood. When the boy had come near he asked where he should put the wood. At first the father was too much frightened to reply, but at last he told his son to put the wood down near the house.

For a long time Juan lived at home, but his parents hated him continually, and at last decided to give him poison. One day they sent him on a long trip, giving him seven pieces of poisoned bread for his food along the way. When he had become weary and hungry from walking, he sat down under a tree and began to open the handkerchief to get from it some of the bread to eat. Suddenly a number of crows flew down from the tree, seized the bread, ate it, and almost immediately died. The boy at once perceived the intention of his parents and returned home. As soon as he arrived there, he declared to his father and mother his intention of leaving them and going elsewhere to live. As soon as they heard him, they were full of joy, and readily gave him the desired permission.

He went to a distant town, and decided to study. He made such progress that his teachers were charmed with his diligence. He was very fond of debates with his schoolmates, and one day asked them the following riddle: "Two tried to kill one, one killed seven, two were left, and one went away." They searched through the books for the answer to the riddle, but as they were unable to find it, they agreed that Juan was the cleverest one among them, since they could not answer his riddle.

One day the student met a young lady to whom he gave the riddle. She asked for a little time in which to study it, and this being granted, went home, disguised herself as a young man and, returning, asked Juan to tell the answer to the riddle. "For I know," she said, "that many students have tried to find the solution of this riddle, but have not been successful." Juan finally granted her request, and told her the answer to the riddle, which was the story of his life.

Then the young lady returned home, put on her own clothes, and went back to the student's house, to give him the answer to his riddle. When Juan heard her answer, he thought her a very clever young woman, since she had succeeded where so many young men had failed, so he fell in love with the young lady and married her.

The Two Wives and the Witch.

There was once a man who had a wife that was not pretty. He became tired of looking at her, and so went away and married another wife.

His first wife was in great sorrow, and wept every day. One day as she was crying by the well, where she had gone for water, a woman asked her: "Why are you weeping?" The wife answered: "Because my husband has left me and gone to live with another wife." "Why?" said the witch, for that is what the woman was.

"Because I have not a pretty face," answered the wife. While she was talking the witch touched the wife's face, and then she said: "I cannot stay here any longer," and went off.

When the wife reached home she looked in the glass and saw that her face had been changed until it was the most beautiful in the town. Very soon a rumor spread through the town that in such and such a house there was living a very beautiful woman. Many young men went to see the pretty woman, and all were pleased with her beauty.

The bad husband went also. He was astonished that his wife was not at home, and that a pretty woman was living there alone. He bowed to the lady and avowed his love. The lady at first refused to believe him, and said: "If you will leave the woman who is now your wife and come to live with me right along I will take you for my husband." The man agreed, and went to live with the pretty woman.

The other woman was very angry when she heard the news, for it was reported that the pretty woman was the man's first wife, who had been changed by a witch. She determined to try what the witch could do for her, and went to get water at the same well.

The witch appeared and asked: "Why are you weeping, my good woman?" The woman told her that her husband had gone away to live with the pretty woman. As she was speaking, the witch touched her face, and said: "Go home, my good woman, and do not weep, for your husband will come very soon to see you."

When she heard this she ran home as fast as she could. All the people whom she met on the road were afraid of her, because she was so ugly. Her nose was about two feet long, her ears looked like large handkerchiefs, and her eyes were as big as saucers. Nobody recognized her, not even her mother. All were afraid of such a creature. When she saw in the glass how ugly she was, she refused to eat, and in a few days she died.

The Living Head.

There once lived a man and his wife who had no children. They earnestly desired to have a son, so they prayed to their God, Diva, that he would give them a son, even if it were only a head.

Diva pitied them, and gave them a head for a son. Head, for that was his name, grew up, and gradually his father and mother ceased to think of his misfortune, and grew to love him very much.

One day Head saw the chief's daughter pass the house, and fell in love with her. "Mother," he said, "I am in love with the chief's daughter and wish to marry her. Go now, I pray you, to the chief and ask him to give me his daughter to be my wife." "Dear Head," answered his mother, "it is of no use to go on such an errand, the chief's daughter will surely not be willing to marry only a head." But Head insisted, so, in order to quiet him, his mother went to the chief and made known her son's desire. Of course she met with a refusal, and returned home and told Head the result of her errand.

Head went downstairs into the garden and began to sink into the ground.

"Head, come up," said his mother, "and let us eat."

"Sink! sink! sink!" cried Head.

"Head, come up and let us eat!" repeated his mother.

"Sink! sink! sink!" was Head's answer, and he continued to sink until he could no longer be seen. His mother tried in vain to take him out. After a while a tree sprang up just where Head had sunk, and in a short time it bore large, round fruit, almost as large as a child's head. This is the origin of the orange-tree.

Juan Pusong.

The Visayans tell many stories which have as their hero Juan Pusong, or Tricky John. As the name implies, he is represented as being deceitful and dishonest, sometimes very cunning, and, in some of the stories told of him, endowed with miraculous power. The stories are very simple and of not very great excellence. The few which follow will serve as samples of the narratives told of this popular hero.

I. Juan Pusong was a lazy boy. Neither punishment nor the offer of a reward could induce him to go to school, but in school-time he was always to be found on the plaza, playing with the other boys.

His mother, however, believed him to be in school, and each day prepared some dainty for him to eat upon his return home. Juan was not satisfied with deceiving his mother in this way, but used to play tricks on her.

"Mother," he said, one day, "I have already learned to be a seer and to discover what is hidden. This afternoon when I come home from school I will foretell what you have prepared for me."

"Will you?" said his mother joyfully, for she believed all he said, "I will try to prepare something new and you will not be able to guess it."

"I shall, mother, I shall, let it be whatever it may," answered Juan. When it was time to go to school, Juan pretended to set out, but instead he climbed a tree which stood near the kitchen, and hiding himself among the leaves, watched through the window all that his mother did.

His mother baked a bibingca, or cake made of rice and sweet potato, and hid it in a jar. "I will bet anything," she said, "that my son will not guess what it is." Juan laughed at his mother's self-conceit. When it was time for school to close he got down, and with a book in his hand, as though he had really come from school, appeared before his mother and said: "Mother, I know what you are keeping for me."

"What is it?" asked his mother.

"The prophecy that I have just learned at school says that there is a bibingca hidden in the olla." The mother became motionless with surprise. "Is it possible?" she asked herself, "my son is indeed a seer. I am going to spread it abroad. My son is a seer."

The news was spread far and wide and many people came to make trial of Pusong's powers. In these he was always successful, thanks to his ability to cheat.

II. One day a ship was anchored in the harbor. She had come from a distant island. Her captain had heard of Pusong's power and wished to try him. The trial consisted in foretelling how many seeds the oranges with which his vessel was loaded contained. He promised to give Juan a great quantity of money if he could do this.

Pusong asked for a day's time. That night he swam out to the vessel, and, hidden in the water under the ship's stern, listened to the conversation of the crew. Luckily they were talking about this very matter of the oranges, and one of them inquired of the captain what kind of oranges he had.

"My friend," said the captain, "these oranges are different from any in this country, for each contains but one seed."

Pusong had learned all that he needed to know, so he swam back to the shore, and the next morning announced that he was ready for the trial.

Many people had assembled to hear the great seer. Pusong continued to read in his book, as though it was the source of his information. The hour agreed upon struck, and the captain of the vessel handed an orange to Juan and said: "Mr. Pusong, you may tell us how many seeds this orange contains."

Pusong took the orange and smelled it. Then he opened his book and after a while said: "This orange you have presented me with contains but one seed."

The orange was cut and but the one seed found in it, so Pusong was paid the money. Of course he obtained a great reputation throughout the country, and became very rich.

III. Juan Pusong's father drove his cows out one day to pasture. Juan slipped secretly from the house, and going to the pasture, took the cows into the forest and tied them there. When his father was going for the cows he met Juan and asked: "Where did you come from?" The boy replied: "I have just come from school. What are you looking for?"

"I am looking for our cows," said his father.

"Why did n't you tell me that before," asked Juan. "Wait a minute," and he took his little book from his pocket and, looking into it, said: "Our cows are in such a place in the forest, tied together. Go and get them." So his father went to the place where Juan said the cows were and found them. Afterwards it was discovered that Juan could not read even his own name, so his father beat him for the trick he had played.

IV. Pusong and Tabloc-laui. Pusong had transgressed the law, and was for this reason put into a cage to be in a short time submerged with it into the sea.

Tabloc-laui, a friend of Pusong's, passed by and saw him in the cage. "What are you there for?" Tabloc-laui asked.

"Oh!" answered Pusong, "I am a prisoner here, as you see, because the chief wants me to marry his daughter and I don't want to do it. I am to stay here until I consent."

"What a fool you are!" said Tabloc-laui. "The chief's daughter is pretty, and I am surprised that you are not willing to marry her."

"Hear me, Tabloc-laui!" said the prisoner. "If you want to marry the chief's daughter, let me out and get in here in my place; for tomorrow they will come and ask you if you will consent. Then you will be married at once."

"I am willing!" exclaimed Tabloc-laui. "Get out and I will take your place!"

Next morning the chief ordered his soldiers to take the cage with the prisoner to the sea and submerge it in the water.

Tabloc-laui, on seeing the soldiers coming toward him, thought they would make inquiries of him as Pusong had said.

"I am ready now," he said, "I am ready to be the princess's husband."

"Is this crazy fellow raving?" asked the soldiers. "We are ordered to take you and submerge you in the sea."

"But," objected Tabloc-laui, "I am ready now to marry the chief's daughter."

He was carried to the sea and plunged into the water, in spite of his crying, "I am not Pusong! I am Tabloc-laui!"

The next week the chief was in his boat, going from one fish-trap to another, to inspect them. Pusong swam out to the boat.

The chief, on seeing him, wondered, for he believed that Pusong was dead. "How is this?" he asked. "Did you not drown last week?"

"By no means. I sank to the bottom, but I found that there was no water there. There is another world where the dead live again. I saw your father and he charged me to bid you go to him, and afterwards you will be able to come back here, if you wish to do so." "Is that really true, Pusong?" asked the chief. "Yes, it is really true," was the reply.

"Well, I will go there. I will have a cage made and go through the way you did."

So the next morning the chief was submerged in the water, with the hope of coming back. When a considerable time had elapsed without seeing his return, his servants searched for Pusong, in order to punish him, but he had escaped to the mountains.

V. The Enchanted Prince. There was once a king who had three young and beautiful daughters named Isabel, Catalina, and Maria.

In the capital city of the kingdom lived a young man known by the name of Juan Pusong. He had as friends an ape, named Amo-Mongo, and a wildcat, whose name was Singalong. The three friends were passing one day in front of the palace, and, seeing the three young ladies, were greatly charmed by their beauty.

Pusong, who posed as a young aristocrat of considerable learning, determined to go before the king and declare his love for the Princess Isabel. The king received him favorably, and offered him a seat; but Juan refused to sit down until he should know the result of his request.

The king was astonished at his manner, and asked him what he wanted. Juan replied that he had presumptuously allowed himself to be charmed by the beauty of the Princess Isabel, and humbly requested the king's consent to their marriage. The king had the princess summoned before him, and in the presence of Pusong asked her if she would accept this man as her husband. She dutifully expressed her willingness to do whatever her father wished, so the king granted the request of Pusong, who was immediately married to Isabel.

When Amo-Mongo saw how successful Pusong had been, he presented himself before the king, as his friend had done, and requested the hand of the Princess Catalina. The king, somewhat unwillingly, gave his consent, and these two were also married.

When Singalong saw to what high positions his friends had attained, he became desirous of like fortune, so he went to the king and obtained his consent to his marriage with the Princess Maria.

All three of the king's sons-in-law lived with their wives at the palace, at the king's expense. The latter seeing that his daughters' husbands were lazy fellows, determined to make them useful, so he sent Pusong and Amo-Mongo out to take charge of his estates in the country, while to Singalong he gave the oversight of the servants who worked in the kitchen of the palace.

Pusong and Amo-Mongo went out to the hacienda with the intention of doing something, but when they arrived there, they found so much to do that they concluded that it would be impossible to attend to everything and so decided to do nothing.

The latter, after merely looking over the estate, entered the forest, in order to visit his relatives there. His fellow monkeys, who knew of his marriage with the princess, believed him to be of some importance, and begged him to save them from the famine which was devastating the forest. This

Amo-Mongo, with much boasting of his wealth, promised to do, declaring that at the time of harvest he would give them plenty of rice.

When Pusong and his companion returned to the palace they were asked by the king how many acres they had cleared. They replied that they had cleared and planted about one thousand acres. The king was satisfied with their answer, and, at Amo-Mongo's request, gave orders for a large quantity of rice to be carried from the storehouse to the spot in the forest where his son-in-law had promised the monkeys that they should find it.

On the other hand, Singalong during the day did nothing, and as the king never saw him at work he disliked his third son-in-law very much. Yet every morning there were great piles of fish and vegetables in the palace kitchen. Amo-Mongo, knowing that his brother-in-law usually went out at night in order to bring something home, contrived to get up early and see what there was in the kitchen, so as to present it to the king as the result of his own labors. In this way, Amo-Mongo became each day dearer and dearer to the king, while Singalong became more and more disliked. Maria knew that her husband procured their food in some way, for every morning he said to her: "All that you see here I have brought." However, the king knew nothing of all this.

When the early harvest time came, the king commanded Amo-Mongo to bring rice to make pilipig. (Rice pounded into flakes and toasted, a dish of which Filipinos are very fond.) Amo-Mongo did not know where he could find it, but set out in the direction from which he had seen Singalong coming each morning, and soon came to an extensive rice-field bearing an abundant crop. He took a goodly portion of it and, returning to the palace, had the pilipig prepared and set before the king and his household. Every one ate of it, except Singalong, who was the real owner, and his wife, who had been secretly notified by him of the truth of the matter.

Maria was greatly perplexed by what her husband had told her, so she determined one night to watch him. She discovered that, as soon as the other people were asleep, her husband became transformed into a handsome prince and left the palace, leaving behind him his cat's dress. As soon as he had gone, Maria took the cast-off clothing of her husband and cast it into the fire. Singalong smelt it burning and returned to the palace, where he found his wife and begged her to return to him his cat's dress. This she was unable to do, since it was entirely consumed. As a result, Singalong was obliged to retain the form of a prince, but he was afraid to appear before the king in this guise, and so hid himself.

In the morning, Maria went to the king and told him the truth about her husband. Her father, however, thought that she was crazy, and when she insisted, invited her to accompany him to Amo-Mongo's farm, in order to convince her of her error. Many people went with them, and Amo-Mongo led them to the farm, which was really Singalong's, but told them that it belonged to himself. Besides other things, Singalong had planted many fruits, among them atimon and candol.

Amo-Mongo, seeing the diversity of fruits, began to eat all he could, until he became unable to move a step. Whenever his wife urged him to come away, he would take an atimon under his arm and a candol or so in his hands, until at last his wife, angry at his greediness, gave him a push which caused him to fall headlong, striking his head against a stone and being instantly killed.

Then Singalong, who had secretly followed the crowd from the palace, showed himself to the king in his proper form. After making suitable explanations, he led them to a fine palace in the middle of the hacienda. There they all lived together, but Pusong and his wife, who in former times had treated

Singalong very harshly, giving him only the bones and scraps from the table, were now obliged to act as servants in the kitchen of the king's new palace.

The Enchanted Ring.

There was once a king who had suffered for a long time with a painful disease, in spite of all the efforts of the doctors to cure it. At last he caused a proclamation to be made that whoever could cure him should marry his daughter as a reward.

One day a snake appeared before the king and asked permission to cure him. The king at first refused, but the snake said that his body contained some gall whose power to cure was wonderful, so the king consented to try it, and was soon cured.

The snake was really a prince who had been changed into this form by enchantment. Every night he took on his proper form and went for a walk around the city. His wife once saw him do this, so she asked him to tell her the truth. The snake told her his secret, but forbade her to tell any one, on pain of his leaving her.

One day the other daughters of the king consulted as to how they should find out the truth about their sister's husband. They took their sister into the garden and asked her many questions, but Maria kept silent about the snake's secret. So her sisters fastened her to a tree at the bottom of which was an ant's nest. Maria could not long endure the pain of the bites of the ants and told her sisters the truth. They let her go back home, but she could not find her husband anywhere, and set out to look for him. She asked the birds she met if they had seen him, but they answered that they had flown over all the country around, for hundreds of miles, without seeing him. She was very sorrowful, and at last, worn out with grief and weariness, lay down to sleep under a tree which was barren of leaves, except for three large ones at the very top.

Maria dreamed that her husband was in a house not far away and was dangerously ill. She dreamed, also, that the leaves on the top of the tree under which she was sleeping were the only cure for his sickness. As soon as she awoke, she climbed the tree and got the leaves and took them with her to the house, where she found her husband, just as she had dreamed.

When she came to the door of the house she met a black woman whom she asked about Don Juan, which was the prince's name. The black woman told her that he was sick, and asked her why she had come. Maria replied that she had learned of his sickness and had come to cure him with some leaves. As soon as the negress learned about the leaves, she took them and gave them to the prince, who immediately recovered from his sickness.

The prince had promised to marry any woman who could cure him, and as the black woman had cured him he married her. The negress, seeing that she was ugly, tried to make Maria so also, so she took her as a servant and painted her black; but Maria had an enchanted ring which gave her the power of changing her form. Every night in her room Maria made use of her ring, obtaining by means of it her maids of honor, fine dresses, and a band which played sweet music.

It chanced one night that Don Juan was awakened by the sound of music. He traced it to a certain room, and looking through the keyhole, saw all that was going on in Maria's room. He was greatly astonished and stood watching for a long time. Suddenly he saw Maria take from her ring a pair of scissors. These at a sign suspended themselves in the air, ready, when Maria should give the signal, to fall and pierce her heart. Don Juan rushed into the room and caught the scissors just as they were falling.

Then Maria told him all that had happened to her. She was proclaimed as the prince's true wife, and the black woman was put to death as a punishment for her deception.

The Enchanted Shell.

In the olden time there lived a man and his wife who had no son. They prayed that they might have a son, even if he were only like a little shell. When their son was born, he was very small, and just like a shell, so he was named Shell.

One day Shell asked permission of his mother to go and get some food. His mother at first would not let him, as she was afraid he would meet some animal which would kill him; but at last she consented, and he set out.

He went to the river, where some women were catching fish and putting them into baskets. One of them laid her basket on the grass near the river and Shell crept into it. In a few minutes the woman picked up her basket and started for home. All at once Shell began to cry "Rain! Rain!" The woman was so frightened at hearing the fishes talk, as she supposed, that she threw down her basket and ran away. Then Shell took the basket full of fish to his mother.

The next day Shell went out again. He saw an old man walking along the road and carrying the head of a cow, so he followed him. The old man went into the house of a friend, leaving the cow's head hanging on the fence. Shell climbed up the fence and got into the cow's ear, keeping very quiet. When the old man came out of the house he took the head and continued his walk. As he reached a desert place called Cahana-an, the head began to say: "Ay! Ay!" The old man became so frightened that he threw the head away, and Shell carried it home.

Days passed. Shell told his mother that he was in love with a beautiful daughter of the chief and must have her for his wife. The poor mother was amazed and did not want to present his request to the chief. "My dear Shell," she said, "you are beside yourself." But he urged her and urged her, until at last she went. She begged the chief's pardon for her boldness and made known her errand. The chief was astonished, but agreed to ask his daughter if she were willing to take Shell for a husband. Much to his surprise and anger she stated that she was willing to marry him. Her father was so enraged that he exclaimed: "I consider you as being lower than my servants. If you marry this Shell I will drive you out of the village." But Shell and the girl were married, and escaped from the town to a little house in the fields, where they lived in great sorrow for a week. But at the end of that time, one night at midnight, the shell began to turn into a good-looking man, for he had been enchanted at his birth by an evil spirit. When his wife saw how handsome he was, she was very glad, and afterwards the chief received them back into his favor.

The Three Brothers.

Once upon a time there was a great king who had three sons. The oldest was named Pedro, the next Pablo, and the youngest Juan. One day their father called them to him, and giving each one a small sum of money, said: "Go and seek for yourselves wives, for I am getting old and wish to see you settled down before I die. The one who gets the most beautiful wife shall have the kingdom. In addition to the money I have given you, you may each have a horse from my stables."

Pedro and Pablo rushed off and secured the best horses, so that when Juan, who had stopped to thank his father, arrived at the stable, he found only an old horse, scarcely able to walk. However, he determined to set out; but after getting a mile or so from home, he saw that it was impossible to go farther, so sat down on a well-curb and wept bitterly. While he was weeping, a frog floated to the top of the water and asked what the matter was, and Juan told him all about his trouble. The frog said: "Never mind. Go to sleep for an hour and I will look for a wife for you."

At the end of the hour the frog awoke Juan and said: "Go home now, and tell your father that you have found a wife." Juan did so, and found his brothers at home, each claiming to have found a wife. Their father said: "I wish to test your wives. Here are three handkerchiefs. Each of you must take one of them to his bride and have it embroidered." They took the handkerchiefs and departed; but Juan, when he had arrived at the well, sat down as before and wept, because he thought that now he would surely be found out.

The frog floated again to the surface of the well and asked Juan what the matter was. Juan replied, "I told my father that I had found a wife, as you bade me, and now he wishes to test my wife, to see if she is a suitable mate for me, and has sent me with this handkerchief for her to embroider. I do not know what to do, for now my father will surely find out that I have deceived him, and I shall be disgraced." The frog said: "Do not worry. Give me your handkerchief and go to sleep for an hour and I will have it embroidered for you." At the end of the hour the frog brought to Juan the handkerchief, all beautifully embroidered. When Juan arrived at home, he found his brothers there, each with his handkerchief beautifully embroidered, but Juan's handkerchief was embroidered the most beautifully of all.

Then their father said: "Your wives, evidently, can embroider well, but I must see how they can cook. Here are three cows. Each of you must take one of them and have your wife cook it." The brothers went off with the cows, but Juan led his cow to the well in which the frog lived, and, as before, sat down and began to weep. After a while the frog came to the top of the water and asked: "Why are you weeping so bitterly?" "Oh, my dear frog! Here is a cow which my father says my wife must cook. What shall I do?" The frog replied: "Go to sleep for an hour and I will cook the meat for you." Juan went to sleep, and at the end of the hour the frog woke him, and showing him the cow cooked whole, said: "Take this home and when you have carried it upstairs, break off one horn and see what will happen." Juan took the roast cow home, and when he arrived there found his brothers before him, with their meat roasted. Juan carried his cow upstairs and each animal was placed upon a table by itself. The king tasted Pedro's meat, and found it too salt. Then he tried Pablo's, and found it not salt enough. When he approached the table on which Juan's meat was laid, Juan broke off one of the cow's horns, and immediately a beautiful service of silver dishes, enough for twelve persons, rolled out, each dish taking its proper place upon the table, with the roast cow in the midst. Then the king and his councillors sat down to the feast, and when they had tasted the meat, they found it just right.

On the next day the king ordered his sons to bring their wives to the palace, so that he might decide which was the most beautiful. Juan was in more trouble than ever, for now he was sure of being discovered; so he went to the well again, weeping bitterly and calling aloud for the frog. In a few minutes the frog appeared, and to him Juan related his trouble. The frog said: "Under that tree is a hammock; go to sleep in it for an hour, and three women will wake you by shaking the hammock. Take the middle one and return home, for that one is to be your wife." All happened as the frog had said. Juan took the woman home with him, and as he approached the house, his father was looking out of the window. When the king saw how beautiful Juan's wife was, he was so overcome with joy that he fainted. When he had recovered, he declared Juan's wife was the most beautiful woman he had ever seen. So to Juan was given the kingdom. Pedro became the palace coachman, and Pablo the cook.

Berton L. Maxfield, Ph. B.

Brooklyn, N. Y.

The Datto Somacuel.

Datto Somacuel was one of the seven chiefs who, coming from Borneo many years before the Spaniards conquered these islands, settled the Island of Panay. He lived in Sinaragan, a town near San Joaquin, in the southern part of Iloilo Province. His wife's name was Capinangan.

Somacuel went every morning to the seashore to watch his slaves fish with the sinchoro, or net. One day they caught many fishes, and Somacuel commanded them:—

"Spread the fish to dry, and take care that the crows do not eat them up."

A slave answered: "Sir, if your treasure inside the house is stolen by the crows, how do you expect those out of doors to be kept safe?" This was said with a certain intonation that made Somacuel conjecture that there was a hidden meaning in it.

"What do you mean by that?" he asked.

"Sir, I have to inform you of something that I should have told you long ago. Do not reprove me if I have been backward in telling you of the injury done you by your wife. It was due to my desire to get complete proofs of the truth of my statement."

"End at once your tedious narrative!" said the datto, "What did my wife do?"

"Sir," answered the slave, "she deceives you shamefully. She loves Gorong-Gorong, who is at this very moment in your house jesting at your absence."

"Alas!" said Somacuel, "if this be true he shall pay well for his boldness."

The chief hurried home, intending to surprise the offenders. He carried a fish called ampahan in a bamboo tube full of water, going around by a secret way, so as not to be seen. On reaching home he went up into the attic to observe what was going on, and found that his informant had told the truth.

Gorong-Gorong and Capinangan were engaged in an affectionate dialogue. Involuntarily Somacuel spilled some of the water down, and, fearing that he would be discovered, seized a spear that was hidden in the attic and, dropping it down, dexterously ran Gorong-Gorong through the body, killing him instantly.

"Oh, Diva!" exclaimed Capinangan, kneeling beside the inert corpse,

"How shall I be able to take it away without being discovered by

Somacuel?"

Somacuel, who had not been seen at all, stayed quietly above, watching what Capinangan would do. Capinangan did not suspect that her husband was there, as he usually did not come home before nightfall. She tried to take the corpse out for burial, but could not carry the heavy body of her unfortunate lover. She must conceal it in some way, and it was dangerous for her to call for aid, lest she might be betrayed to her husband. So she took a knife and cut the body into pieces so that she could take them out and bury them under the house.

After this task was done she managed to wash the blood up. She became tranquil for a moment, believing she would never be discovered. Somacuel, however, had observed all, and he formed a plan for punishing his wife as she deserved. When everything seemed to be calm he crept down, doing his best not to be seen. At the door he called his wife by name. Capinangan was afraid, but concealed her fear with a smile. "Capinangan," said her husband, "cut this fish in pieces and cook it for me."

Capinangan was astonished at this command, because she had never before been treated in this way. They had many slaves to perform such tasks.

"You know I cannot," she said.

"Why not?" asked her husband.

"Because I have never learned how to cut a fish in pieces nor to cook it," she replied.

"I am astonished that you don't know how to cut, after seeing that cutting is your favorite occupation," said Somacuel.

Capinangan then did not doubt that her husband knew what she had done, so she did as he had bidden.

When dinner was ready the husband and wife ate it, but without speaking to each other. After the meal, Somacuel told his wife that he had seen all and should punish her severely. Capinangan said nothing. A guilty person has no argument with which to defend himself. Somacuel ordered his servants to throw Capinangan into the sea. At that time the chief's will was law. Neither pleadings nor tears softened his hard heart, and Capinangan was carried down to the sea and thrown in.

Time passed by; Somacuel each day grew sadder and gloomier. He would have been willing now to forgive his wife, but it was too late.

He said to his slaves: "Prepare a banca for me, that I may sail from place to place to amuse myself."

So one pleasant morning a banca sailed from Sinaragan, going southward. Somacuel did not intend to go to any definite place, but drifted at the mercy of wind and current. He amused himself by singing during the voyage.

One day the crew descried land at a distance. "Sir," they said, "that land is Cagayan. Let us go there to get oysters and crane's eggs." To this their master agreed, and upon anchoring off the coast he prepared to visit the place.

Oh, what astonishment he felt, as he saw, peeping out of the window of a house, a woman whose appearance resembled in great measure that of Capinangan! He would have run to embrace her, had he not remembered that Capinangan was dead. He was informed that the woman was named Aloyan. He began to pay court to her, and in a few weeks she became his wife.

Somacuel was happy, for his wife was very affectionate. Aloyan, on her part, did not doubt that her husband loved her sincerely, so she said to him:—

"My dear Somacuel, I will no longer deceive you. I am the very woman whom you caused to be thrown into the sea. I am Capinangan. I clung to a log in the water and was carried to this place, where I have lived ever since."

"Oh," said Somacuel, "pardon me for the harshness with which I meant to punish you."

"Let us forget what is passed," said Capinangan. "I deserved it, after all."

So they returned to Sinaragan, where they lived together happily for many years.

Magbolotó.

There was once a man named Magbolotó who lived in the depths of the mountains. One day on going down to a brook he saw three goddesses bathing in the water. They had left their wings on the bank, and Magbolotó managed to slip down and steal one pair of them. When the goddesses had finished bathing and looked for their wings, they could not find those belonging to the youngest, Macaya. At last the two goddesses put on their wings and flew up to heaven, leaving behind them Macaya, who wept bitterly, since without her wings she could not go home. Then Magbolotó, feigning to have come from a distance, met her and asked: "Why do you weep, lady?"

"Why do you ask, if you will not help me in my trouble?" answered

Macaya.

"I will do my best to help you," said Magbolotó, "if you will tell me about it."

So Macaya told him that she had lost her wings, and therefore could not return to her home in heaven.

"I am sorry not to be able to help you out of your trouble," said Magbolotó, "but we terrestrial people do not use wings, nor know where to get them. The only thing I can do for you is to offer you a home with me." Macaya was obliged to accept his offer, since there was nothing else for her to do.

About a year after Macaya became Magbolotó's wife they had a child. One day, as Magbolotó was making rice soup on the hearth, Macaya was swinging the child in a hammock. Accidentally, she noticed a bundle stuck into one of the bamboo posts in the partition. She withdrew the bundle, and upon unrolling it found, oh, joy! her long-lost wings, which Magbolotó had hidden in the hollow bamboo. She at once put them on, and leaving her husband and child, flew up to join her celestial family.

Magbolotó, on missing his wife, began calling loudly for her. As he could not find her, he looked for the wings, and seeing that they were gone, knew at once what had happened. He began to weep bitterly, especially as he did not know how to take care of the child. So leaving it in the care of a relative, he set out to find the way to heaven. He had walked a great distance when he met North Wind. "Magbolotó, Magbolotó, why are you weeping?" asked North Wind.

"Ask me nothing, if you cannot help me in any way," answered Magbolotó.

"Tell me your trouble and I will help you," said North Wind. "Well," replied Magbolotó, "I have a wife who came from heaven. But now she has flown away, leaving a little child for me to take care of, and I am in great sorrow. Please show me the way that leads to her home."

"Magbolotó," said North Wind, "I do not know the way, but my brother, East Wind, can tell you. Good-by."

Magbolotó went on his way, and after a while he met East Wind. "Magbolotó, Magbolotó, why are you weeping?" asked East Wind.

"Ask me nothing, if you cannot help me in any way," said Magbolotó.

"Tell me all your trouble and I will help you," answered East Wind.

Then Magbolotó related all his sorrow, just as he had done to North Wind.

"Well," said East Wind, "I do not know the way, but my brother, South Wind, may be able to show it to you. Good-by."

Magbolotó went on, and at last met South Wind.

"Magbolotó, Magbolotó, why are you weeping?" asked South Wind.

"Ask me nothing, if you cannot help me in any way," said Magbolotó.

"Tell me your trouble and I will help you," answered South Wind.

Then Magbolotó told him his story, just as he had done to North Wind and East Wind.

"Well," said South Wind, "I do not know the way to heaven, but my brother, West Wind, can tell you the course to be taken to get there. Good-by."

Magbolotó went on and on, and at last met West Wind. "Magbolotó, Magbolotó, why are you weeping?" asked West Wind.

"Ask me nothing, if you cannot help me in any way," answered Magbolotó.

"Tell me your trouble and I will help you," answered West Wind, and Magbolotó did as he was bidden.

"Magbolotó," said West Wind, "I don't know the way to heaven, but my friend, Mr. Eagle, does. Good-by."

Magbolotó went on until he met Mr. Eagle.

"Magbolotó, Magbolotó, why are you weeping?" asked Mr. Eagle.

"Ask me nothing, if you cannot help me in any way," answered Magbolotó.

"Tell me your trouble and I will help you," replied Mr. Eagle. Then Magbolotó told Mr. Eagle his trouble.

"Magbolotó," said Mr. Eagle, "get upon my back and I will carry you to your wife's home."

Magbolotó climbed upon Mr. Eagle's back and they flew up until they reached Macaya's house. Then Magbolotó requested Macaya's grandmother, with whom she lived, to let her granddaughter return to earth with him.

"By no means," said the grandmother, "unless you will spread ten jars of luñga (a certain very small grain) out to dry and gather them again in the evening."

So Magbolotó spread the jars of luñga on the sand, and at noon began to gather them up; but sunset had come before he had gathered more than five handfuls, so he sat down and began to cry like a little boy.

The king of the ants heard him, and wishing to help him, asked:—"Magbolotó, Magbolotó, why are you weeping?"

"Ask me nothing, if you cannot help me."

"Tell me about it and I will help you."

So Magbolotó told the king of the ants all his history, and the condition imposed by the grandmother before he could have his wife, and how impossible it was to fulfil it.

"Well, Magbolotó, you shall be helped," said the king of the ants. Then he blew his horn, and in a little while all his subjects came, and began picking up the grain and putting it into the jars. In a few moments all the grain was in the jars.

The next morning Magbolotó went to get his wife, but the grandmother stopped him, saying:—

"You shall not take my granddaughter away until you have first hulled a hundred bushels of rice."

Magbolotó was in despair, for he knew that to hull one hundred bushels of rice would take him not less than one hundred days, and the grandmother required him to do it in one day; so he cried like a child at his misfortune. The king of the rats heard him crying, and at once came to help him.

"Magbolotó, Magbolotó, why are you weeping?" asked King Rat.

"Ask me nothing, if you cannot help me."

"Relate the matter, and I will."

Magbolotó told him his trouble. Then the king of the rats called his subjects together and ordered them to gnaw the hulls from the rice. In an instant the rice was all hulled.

The next morning Magbolotó made ready to depart with his wife, but the grandmother stopped him again, saying:—

"You may not go until you have chopped down all the trees you see on that mountain over there."

There were more than a million trees, so Magbolotó was in great trouble, and as usual he began to weep.

The king of the wild boars heard him and came up, saying:—

"Magbolotó, Magbolotó, why are you weeping?"

"Ask me nothing, if you cannot help me."

"Relate the matter, and I will."

Magbolotó related all that had happened to him. Then the king of the wild boars called all his subjects together and set them at work cutting down the trees with their tusks. In a few minutes the trees were all down.

When the grandmother saw that Magbolotó accomplished every task she gave him to do she became tired of trying to think of things for him to do; so she allowed him to depart with Macaya, and leaving the celestial abode they descended to their home on the earth, where they lived happily together for many years.

Why Dogs Wag Their Tails.

Once upon a time there lived in a certain pueblo a rich man who had a dog and a cat. His only daughter, of whom he was very fond, was studying in a convent in a city several miles distant and it was his custom, about once a week, to send the dog and cat to take her a little present. The dog was so old that he had lost all his teeth, and so was unable to fight, but the cat was strong and very cunning, and so one could help the other, since the dog knew better how to find the way.

One day the rich man wished to send a magic ring to his daughter, so he called the dog and the cat to him. To the cat he said: "You are very cunning and prudent. You may carry this magic ring to my daughter, but be sure to take very great care of it." To the dog he said: "You are to go with the cat to take a magic ring to my daughter. Take care not to lose the way, and see that no one molests the cat." Both animals promised to do their best and set out immediately.

On the way they were obliged to cross a wide and deep river, over which there was no bridge, and as they were unable to find a boat, they determined to swim across it. The dog said to the cat: "Give me the magic ring." "Oh, no," replied the cat. "Did you not hear the master say just what each of us had to do?"

"Yes, but you are not very good at swimming, and may lose the ring, while I am strong and can take good care of it," answered the dog. The cat continued to refuse to disobey its master, until at last the dog threatened to kill it, and it was obliged to intrust the ring to the dog's keeping.

Then they began to swim across the river, which was so strong that they were about an hour in getting over, so that both became very tired and weak. Just before they came to the other side, the dog dropped the ring into the water, and it was impossible to find it. "Now," said the cat, "we had better go back home and tell our master that we have lost the ring." "Yes," answered the dog, "but I am very much afraid." So they turned back toward home, but as they drew near the house his fear so overcame him that he ran away and was never seen again.

The master was very much surprised to see the cat back so soon, and asked him, "Where is your companion?" The cat was at first afraid to answer. "Where is the dog?" asked the master again. "Oh, he ran away," replied the cat. "Ran away?" said the master. "What do you mean? Where is the ring?" "Oh, pardon me, my master," answered the cat. "Do not be angry, and I will tell you what has happened. When we reached the bank of the river, the dog asked me to give him the ring. This I refused many times, until at last he threatened to kill me if I did not give it to him, and I was obliged to do so. The river was very hard to cross, and on the way the dog dropped the ring into the water and we could not find it. I persuaded the dog to come back with me to tell you about it, but on the way he became so frightened that he ran away."

Then the master made a proclamation to the people, offering a reward to the one who should find his old dog and bring him to him. They could recognize the dog by his being old and having no teeth. The master also declared that when he had found the delinquent he would punish him by cutting off his tail. He ordered that the dogs all around the world should take part in the search, and so ever since that time, when one dog meets another he always asks: "Are you the old dog who lost the magic ring? If you are, your tail must be cut off." Then instantly both show their teeth and wag their tails to mean no. Since that time, also, cats have been afraid of water, and will never swim across a river if it can be avoided.

The Eagle and the Hen.

One day the eagle declared his love for the hen. He flew down to search for her, and when he had found her he said: "I wish you to be my mate."

The hen answered: "I am willing, but let me first grow wings like yours, so I can fly as high as you." The eagle replied: "I will do so, and as a sign of our betrothal I will give you this ring. Take good care of it until I come again."

The hen promised to do so, and the eagle flew away.

The next day the cock met the hen. When he saw the ring around her neck he was very much surprised and said: "Where did you get that ring? I think you are not true to me. Do you not remember your promise to be my mate? Throw away that ring." So she did.

At the end of a week the eagle came with beautiful feathers to dress the hen. When she saw him she became frightened and hid behind the door. The eagle entered, crying: "How are you, my dear hen? I am bringing you a beautiful dress," and he showed it to the hen. "But where is your ring? Why do you not wear it?" The hen could not at first answer, but after a little she tried to deceive the eagle, and said: "Oh, pardon me, sir! Yesterday as I was walking in the garden I met a large snake, and I was so frightened that I ran towards the house. When I reached it I found that I had lost the ring, and I looked everywhere for it; but alas! I have not yet found it."

The eagle looked keenly at the hen and said: "I would never have believed that you would behave so badly. I promise you that, whenever you have found my ring, I will come down again and take you for my mate. As a punishment for breaking your promise you shall always scratch the ground and look for the ring, and all your chickens that I find I will snatch away from you. That is all. Good-by." Then he flew away.

And ever since, all the hens all over the world have been scratching to find the eagle's ring.

Note.—The bird of whom this story is told is the dapay, or brahman kite. It is larger than most of our hawks and is more like the eagle in appearance, although not very large.

The Spider and the Fly.

Mr. Spider was once in love with Miss Fly. Several times he declared his love, but was always repelled, for Miss Fly disliked his business.

One day, when she saw him coming, she closed the doors and windows of her house and made ready a pot of boiling water.

Mr. Spider called to be allowed to enter the house, but Miss Fly's only answer was to throw the boiling water at him.

"Well!" cried Mr. Spider, "I and my descendants shall be avenged upon you and yours. We will never give you a moment's peace."

Mr. Spider did not break his word, for to this day we see his hatred of the fly.

The Battle of the Crabs.

One day the land crabs had a meeting. One of them said: "What shall we do with the waves? They sing all the time so loudly that we cannot possibly sleep well at night." "Do you not think it would be well for all of us males to go down and fight them?" asked the eldest of the crabs. "Yes," all replied. "Well, to-morrow all the males must get ready to go."

The next day they started to go down to the sea. On the way they met the shrimp. "Where are you going, my friends?" asked the shrimp. The crabs answered: "We are going to fight the waves, because they will not let us sleep at night."

"I don't think you will win the battle," said the shrimp. "The waves are very strong, while your legs are so weak that your bodies bend almost to the ground when you walk," and he laughed. The crabs were so angry at his scorn that they ran at the shrimp and pinched him until he promised to help them in the battle.

When they reached the shore, the crabs looked at the shrimp and said: "Your face is turned the wrong way, friend shrimp," and they laughed at him, for crabs are much like other people, and think they are the only ones who are right. "Are you ready to fight with the waves? What weapon have you?"

"My weapon," replied the shrimp, "is a spear on my head." Just then he saw a large wave coming, and ran away; but the crabs, who were all looking towards the shore, did not see it, and were killed.

The wives of the dead crabs wondered why their husbands did not come home. They thought the battle must be a long one, and decided to go down and help their husbands. As they reached the shore and entered the water to look for their husbands, the waves killed them.

A short time afterwards, thousands of little crabs, such as are now called fiddlers, were found near the shore. When these children were old enough to walk, the shrimp often visited them and related to them the sad fate of their parents. And so, if you will watch carefully the fiddlers, you will notice that they always seem ready to run back to the land, where their forefathers lived, and then, as they regain their courage, they rush down, as if about to fight the waves. But they always lack the courage to do so, and continually run back and forth. They live neither on dry land, as their ancestors did, nor in the sea, like the other crabs, but up on the beach, where the waves wash over them at high tide and try to dash them to pieces.

The Meeting of the Plants.

Once upon a time plants were able to talk as well as people, and to walk from place to place. One day King Molave, the strongest tree, who lived on a high mountain, called his subjects together for a general meeting.

Then every tree put itself in motion towards the designated spot, each doing its best to reach it first. But the buri palm was several days late, which made the king angry, and he cursed it in these terms:—

"You must be punished for your negligence, and as king I pass upon you this sentence: You shall never see your descendants, for you shall die just as your seeds are ready to grow."

And from that day the buri palms have always died without seeing their descendants.

Who Brings the Cholera?

The Filipinos, being for the most part ignorant of the laws of hygiene, attribute the cholera to any cause rather than the right one. In general, they believe it to be caused by some evil-minded men, who poison the wells, or, sometimes, by evil spirits, as the following story will show.

Tanag was a poor man who lived in a town in the interior of one of the Philippine Islands. He had nothing to eat, nor could he find any work by which he might earn his food, and so he determined to emigrate. At that time the cholera was at its height.

As Tanag was rather old, he walked so slowly that in a day he had gone but three miles. At sunset he was crossing a sheltered bridge over a smooth brook near the sea, and determined to rest and spend the night there.

During the early part of the night he was all right, but later it occurred to him that he might be seen and killed by the ladrones, who often passed that way.

Below the bridge was a raft of bamboo poles, and he thought it would be wise to get down there, where he could not so easily be seen. But there were many mosquitoes over the water, so that he was unable to sleep. He determined, however, to stay there until day dawned.

At about four o'clock he heard a heavy step upon the floor of the bridge, and by the moonlight he could see that the new-comer was a huge giant with a long club.

A little later another giant came, and Tanag, full of fear, heard the following dialogue:—

"Did you kill many people?"

"Yes, I put my poison on the food, and in a short time those who ate of it were attacked by the cholera and died. And how are you getting along yourself?"

"At first I killed many people with my poison, but now I am disappointed, because they have found out the antidote for it."

"What is that?"

"The root of the balingay tree boiled in water. It is a powerful antidote against the poison I use. And what is the antidote against yours?"

"Simply the root of the alibutbut tree boiled in water. Luckily, no one has discovered this antidote, and so many people will die."

In the morning Tanag saw the giants going to the shore, where many people were fishing with their nets. The giants flung their poison on the fish, and then disappeared from Tanag's sight.

Tanag believed that the cholera was caused by the two giants, who poisoned the food and water by sprinkling poison on them, and he did not doubt that the roots of the balingay and alibutbut trees would prove to be the antidotes to the poison. So he gathered the roots and cooked them and advertised himself as a doctor.

In fact he cured many people and earned so much money that he soon became rich.

Masoy and the Ape.

Masoy was a poor man who lived on a farm some miles from the town. His clothing was very poor, and his little garden furnished him scarcely enough to live on. Every week day he went to town to sell his fruits and vegetables and to buy rice. Upon his return he noticed each day that some one had entered the garden in his absence and stolen some of the fruit. He tried to protect the garden by making the fence very strong and locking the gate; but, in spite of all he could do, he continued to miss his fruit.

At length Masoy conceived the happy idea of taking some pitch and moulding it into the shape of a man. He put a bamboo hat on it and stood it up in one comer of the garden. Then he went away.

As soon as he was gone, the robber, who was none other than a huge ape, climbed the fence and got in.

"Oh!" he said to himself, "I made a mistake! There is Masoy watching. He did not go away as I thought. He is here with a big bamboo hat, but he could not catch me if he tried. I am going to greet him, for fear he may consider me impolite."

"Good morning, Masoy," he said. "Why do you not answer me? What is the matter with you? Oh! you are joking, are you, by keeping so silent? But you will not do it again." On saying this, the ape slapped the man of pitch with his right hand, and of course it stuck, and he could not get it loose.

"For heaven's sake," cried the ape, "let me go. If you do not, I will slap you with my other hand." Then he struck him with the other hand, which, of course, stuck fast also.

"Well, Masoy," cried the ape, "you have entirely exhausted my patience! If you don't let go of me at once, I shall kick you." No sooner said than done, with a result which may easily be imagined.

"Masoy," cried the now enraged ape, "if you have any regard for your own welfare, let me go, for if you don't, I still have one leg left to kill you with." So saying, he kicked him with the remaining foot, getting so tangled up that he and the tar man fell to the ground, rolling over and over.

Then Masoy came, and, when he saw the ape, he said: "So you are the robber who has stolen my fruit! Now you will pay for it with your life."

But the ape cried, "Oh, spare my life, and I will be your slave forever!"

"Do you promise not to steal my fruit again?"

"I do, and I will serve you faithfully all my life."

Masoy agreed to spare him.

From that time on the ape worked very hard for his master. He sold the fruit and bought the rice and was honest and industrious. One day, on his way to market, he happened to find a small piece of gold and another of silver. At that time this country was not ruled by any foreign power, but each tribe was governed by its own datto or chief. The chief was naturally the bravest and richest of the tribe.

The chief of Masoy's tribe had a very beautiful daughter. The ape schemed to have her marry his master. Now he hit upon a plan. He went to the chief's house and asked for a ganta, which is a measure holding about three quarts and used for measuring rice.

"My master," he said, "begs you to lend him a ganta to measure his gold with."

The chief was astonished at such an extraordinary request, and asked:

"Who is your master?"

"Masoy, who owns many gantas of gold and silver, acres upon acres of land; and uncountable heads of cattle," was the reply.

The ape carried the ganta home, and there he stuck the piece of gold he had found on the inside of the bottom of the measure, and then returned it to the chief.

"Oh, ape!" said the datto, "your master has forgotten to take out one piece of gold. Take it and give it back to him."

"Never mind, sir," answered the ape, "he has so much gold that that small piece is nothing to him. You may keep it."

Some weeks afterward, the ape went again to borrow the chief's ganta.

"What do you want it for now?" asked the chief.

"To measure my master's silver with," was the answer. So he carried it home, stuck inside the piece of silver he had found, and returned it. The chief found the piece of silver and offered to return it, but was answered as before, that it did not matter.

The chief believed all that the ape said, but was puzzled to know how such a rich man could be living in his territory without his having heard of him.

After a few days the ape, considering the way well prepared for his plans, called upon the datto and said: "My master requests you to give him your daughter in marriage. I am authorized to make all the arrangements with you for the wedding, if you consent to it."

"Very well," answered the chief, "but before we arrange matters I wish to see my future son-in-law. Ask him to come to see me, and I will receive him in a manner befitting his rank."

The ape returned home and said to Masoy, who knew nothing at all of the negotiations with the chief: "I have good news for you. The chief wants to see you, for he intends to give you his daughter in marriage."

"What are you chattering about?" answered Masoy. "Have you lost your senses? Don't you know that I am too poor to marry the chief's daughter? I have not even decent clothes to wear and no means of getting any."

"Do not worry about the clothes. I will get them for you somewhere," replied the ape.

"And how shall I talk? You know that I am ignorant of city ways."

"Oh, Masoy, don't trouble about that! Just answer 'Yes' to the questions they ask you and you will be all right."

Finally Masoy consented to go, and went down to the river to wash off the dirt and grime. A rich merchant was bathing some distance up the river, and the ape slipped along the bank, stole the merchant's clothes, hat, and shoes, and running back swiftly to his master, bade him put them on. Masoy did so, and found himself, for the first time in his life, so well dressed that he no longer hesitated about going to the chief's house. When they arrived there they found that the chief was expecting them and had made a big feast and reception in honor of his future son-in-law. The chief began to talk about the wedding and said:

"Shall we have the wedding in your palace, Masoy?"

"Yes," answered Masoy.

"You have a large palace, I suppose, have n't you, sir?"

"Yes," was the reply.

"Don't you think it would be well for us to go there this afternoon?"

"Yes," was again the reply.

Meanwhile the ape had disappeared. He went along the road towards home and said to all the people he met: "The datto will be along this way pretty soon and when he asks you to whom all these farms and cattle belong, you must say that they are Masoy's, for otherwise he will kill you."

The ape knew that in a certain spot stood an enchanted palace invisible to men. He went to the place, and just where the front of the house appeared whenever it was visible, he began to dig a ditch. The witch who lived in the house appeared and asked: "What are you ditching there for, Mr. Ape?"

"Oh, madam," was his answer, "have n't you heard the news? The chief is coming this way soon, and is going to have all witches and the low animals like myself put to death. For this reason I am digging a pit to hide myself in."

"Oh, Mr. Ape!" said the witch, "let me hide myself first, for I am not able to dig for myself, and you are. Do me this favor, please."

"I should be very impolite, if I refused to do a favor for a lady," said the ape. "Come down, but hurry, or you will be too late."

The witch hurried as fast as she could and got down into the pit. Then the ape threw stones down on her until she was dead. The house then became free from enchantment and always visible.

The ape then returned to the chief's house and reported that all was ready for the wedding. So the chief, Masoy, and the bride, escorted by a large number of people, set out for Masoy's palace. On the way they saw many rich farms and great herds of cattle. The chief asked the people who the owner of these farms and cattle was. The answer always was that they belonged to Masoy. Consequently the chief was greatly impressed by Masoy's great wealth.

The chief greatly admired the palace and considered himself fortunate to have such a son-in-law. That night the wedding took place, and Masoy lived many years in the palace with his wife, having the ape and a great number of slaves to serve him.

Arnomongo and Iput-Iput.

(The Ape and the Firefly.)

One evening the firefly was on his way to the house of a friend, and as he passed the ape's house, the latter asked him: "Mr. Fire-fly, why do you carry a light?" The firefly replied: "Because I am afraid of the mosquitoes." "Oh, then you are a coward, are you?" said the ape. "No, I am not," was the answer. "If you are not afraid," asked the ape, "why do you always carry a lantern?" "I carry a lantern so that when the mosquitoes come to bite me I can see them and defend myself," replied the firefly. Then the ape laughed aloud, and on the next day he told all his neighbors that the firefly carried a light at night because he was a coward.

When the firefly heard what the ape had said, he went to his house. It was night and the ape was asleep, but the firefly flashed his light into his face and awakened him. The firefly was very angry and said: "Why did you spread the report that I was a coward? If you wish to prove which of us is the braver, I will fight you on the plaza next Sunday evening."

The ape inquired: "Have you any companions?" "No," replied the fire-fly, "I will come alone." Then the ape laughed at the idea of such a little creature presuming to fight with him, but the firefly continued: "I shall be expecting you on the plaza about six o'clock next Sunday afternoon." The ape replied: "You had better bring some one to help you, as I shall bring my whole company, about a thousand apes, each as big as myself." This he said, thinking to frighten the strange little insect, who seemed to him to be crazy. But the firefly answered: "I shall not need any companions, but will come alone. Good-by."

When the firefly had gone, the ape called together his company, and told them about the proposed fight. He ordered them to get each one a club about three feet long and to be on the plaza at six o'clock the next Sunday evening. His companions were greatly amazed, but as they were used to obeying their captain, they promised to be ready at the appointed time and place.

On Sunday evening, just before six o'clock, they assembled on the plaza, and found the firefly already waiting for them. Just then the church bells rang the Angelus, so the firefly proposed that they should all pray. Immediately after the prayer, the firefly signified that he was ready to begin. The ape had drawn up his company in line, with himself at the head. Suddenly the firefly lighted upon the ape's nose. The ape next in line struck at the firefly, but succeeded only in striking the captain such a terrible blow on the nose as to kill him. The firefly meanwhile, seeing the blow coming, had jumped upon the nose of the second ape, who was killed by the next in line just as the captain had been killed; and so on down the whole line, until there was but one ape left. He threw down his club and begged the firefly to spare him. The firefly graciously allowed him to live, but since that time the apes have been in mortal terror of the fireflies.

The Snail and the Deer.

The deer made fun of the snail because of his slowness, so the latter challenged the former to a race. "We will race to the well on the other side of the plaza," said the snail. "All right," replied the deer.

On the day of the race the deer ran swiftly to the well, and when he got there he called, "Mr. Snail, where are you?" "Here I am," said the snail, sticking his head up out of the well. The deer was very much surprised, so he said: "I will race you to the next well." "Agreed," replied the snail. When the deer arrived at the next well, he called as before, "Mr. Snail, where are you?" "Here I am," answered the snail. "Why have you been so slow? I have been here a long time waiting for you." The deer tried again and again, but always with the same result; until the deer in disgust dashed his head against a tree and broke his neck.

Now the first snail had not moved from his place, but he had many cousins in each of the wells of the town and each exactly resembled the other. Having heard the crows talking of the proposed race, as they perched on the edge of the wells to drink, they determined to help their cousin to win it, and so, as the deer came to each well, there was always a snail ready to stick his head out and answer, "Here I am" to the deer's inquiry.

Story of Ca Matsin and Ca Boo-Ug.

One day a turtle, whose name was Ca Boo-Ug, and a monkey, Ca Matsin, met on the shore of a pond. While they were talking, they noticed a banana plant floating in the water.

"Jump in and get it," said Ca Matsin, who could not swim, "and we will plant it, and some day we will have some bananas of our own." So Ca Boo-Ug swam out and brought the plant to shore.

"Let's cut it in two," said Ca Matsin. "You may have one half and I will take the other, and then we shall each have a tree."

"All right," said Ca Boo-Ug; "which half will you take?"

Ca Matsin did not think the roots looked very pretty, and so he chose the upper part. Ca Boo-Ug knew a thing or two about bananas, so he said nothing, and each took his part and planted it. Ca Boo-Ug planted his in a rich place in the garden, but Ca Matsin planted his in the ashes in the fireplace, because it was easy, and then, too, he could look at it often and see how pretty it was.

Ca Matsin laughed as he thought how he had cheated Ca Boo-Ug, but soon his part began to wither and die, and he was very angry.

With Ca Boo-Ug it was different. Before long his tree began to put forth leaves, and soon it had a beautiful bunch of bananas on it. But he could not climb the tree to get the bananas, so one day he went in search of Ca Matsin, and asked him how his banana-tree was getting along. When Ca Matsin told him that his tree was dead, Ca Boo-Ug pretended to be very much surprised and sorry, and said:—

"My tree has a beautiful bunch of bananas on it, but I cannot climb up to get them. If you will get some of them for me, I will give you half."

Ca Matsin assented, and climbed the tree. When he got to the top, he pulled a banana, ate it, and threw the skin down to Ca Boo-Ug. Then he ate another, and another, throwing the skins down on Ca Boo-Ug's head. When he had eaten all he wanted, he jumped out of the tree and ran away to the woods, laughing at Ca Boo-Ug. Ca Boo-Ug did not say anything, but just sat down and thought what he should do to get even with Ca Matsin. Finally, he gathered a lot of bamboo sticks and planted them around the tree with the sharp points up, covering them with leaves so that they could not be seen. Then he sat down and waited.

As soon as Ca Matsin got hungry again, he went around to Ca Boo-Ug's garden to get some more bananas. Ca Boo-Ug seemed glad to see him, and when Ca Matsin asked for some bananas, replied:—

"All right, you may have all you want, but on one condition. When you jump out of the tree you must not touch those leaves. You must jump over them."

As soon as Ca Matsin heard that he must not jump on the leaves, that was just what he wanted to do. So when he had eaten all the bananas he wanted, he jumped out of the tree on to the leaves as hard as he could jump, and was killed by the sharp bamboo points.

Then Ca Boo-Ug skinned him and cut him up and packed the meat in a jar of brine and hid it in the mud on the bank of the pond.

In the dry season the banana-trees all died and the cocoanut-trees bore no fruit, so a troop of monkeys came to Ca Boo-Ug and asked him if he would give them something to eat.

"Yes, I have some nice meat in a jar which I will give you, but if

I do, you must promise to eat it with your eyes shut."

They were very hungry, so they gave the required promise, and Ca Boo-Ug gave them the meat. All kept their eyes shut except one, a little baby, and like all babies, he was very curious and wanted to see what was going on. So he opened one eye and peeped at a bone which he had in his hand, then he called out:—

"Oh, see what I have found! Here is the little finger of my brother,

Ca Matsin!"

Then all the monkeys looked, and when they found that Ca Boo-Ug had killed a member of their tribe they were very angry, and looked for Ca Boo-Ug, in order to kill him. But they could not find him, for as soon as he saw what had happened he had hidden under a piece of cocoanut shell which was lying on the ground.

The chief monkey sat upon the cocoanut shell, while he was planning with his companions how they should catch Ca Boo-Ug, but of course he did not know where he was, so he called out: "Where's Ca Boo-Ug? Where's Ca Boo-Ug?"

Ca Boo-Ug was so tickled when he heard the monkey ask where he was that he giggled. The monkeys heard him, and looked all around for him, but could not find him. Then they called out: "Where's Ca Boo-Ug? Where's Ca Boo-Ug?" This time Ca Boo-Ug laughed out loud, and the monkeys found him. Then they began to plan how they should punish him.

"Let's put him into a rice mortar and pound him to death," said one. "Aha!" said Ca Boo-Ug, "that's nothing! My mother beat me so much when I was little that now my back is so strong that nothing can break it."

When the monkeys found out that Ca Boo-Ug was not afraid of being pounded in a rice mortar, they determined to try something else.

"Let's make a fire on his back and burn him up," suggested another. "Oh, ho!" laughed Ca Boo-Ug, "that's nothing. I should think that you could tell by the color of my shell that I have had a fire lighted on my back many times. In fact, I like it, as I am always so cold."

So the monkeys decided that they would punish Ca Boo-Ug by throwing him into the pond and drowning him.

"Boo-hoo!" cried Ca Boo-Ug, "don't do that! You will surely kill me. Please don't do that! Boo-hoo! Boo-hoo!"

Of course when the monkeys found that Ca Boo-Ug did not wish to be thrown into the pond, they thought they had found just the way to kill him. So, in spite of his struggles, they picked him up and threw him far out into the pond.

To their surprise and chagrin, Ca Boo-Ug stuck his head out of the water and laughed at them, and then turned around and swam off.

When the monkeys saw how they had been deceived, they were very much disappointed, and began to plan how they could catch Ca Boo-Ug again. So they called to a big fish, named Botete, that lived in the pond:

"Botete! Drink all you can of the water in the pond and help us find the bag of gold that we hid in it. If you will help us find it, you shall have half of the gold."

So Botete began to drink the water, and in a little time the pond was nearly dry. Then the monkeys determined to go down into the pond and look for Ca Boo-Ug. When he saw them coming, Ca Boo-Ug called to Salacsacan, the kingfisher, who was sitting on a branch of a tree which hung over the water:—

"Salacsacan! Salacsacan! Botete has drunk all the water in the pond, and if there is no water there will be no fish for you to catch. Fly down now and peck a hole in Botete, and let the water out, before the fish are all dead." So Salacsacan flew down and pecked a hole in the side of Botete, and the water rushed out and drowned all the monkeys.

When Ca Boo-Ug saw that the monkeys were all dead, he crawled up on the bank, and there he lived happily ever after.

Another version ends as follows:—

When the monkeys saw how they had been deceived, they were very much disappointed and began to plan how they could catch Ca Boo-Ug again. They decided to drink all the water in the pond, and then they could catch Ca Boo-Ug before he could escape. So they drank and drank, until they all burst.

When Ca Boo-Ug saw that the monkeys were all dead, he crawled up on the bank, and there he lived happily ever after.

W. H. Millington and Berton L. Maxfield.
Brooklyn, N.Y.

PART III

Tagalog Folk-Tales.

Juan Gathers Guavas.

The guavas were ripe, and Juan's father sent him to gather enough for the family and for the neighbors who came to visit them. Juan went to the guava bushes and ate all that he could hold. Then he began to look around for mischief. He soon found a wasp nest and managed to get it into a tight basket. He gave it to his father as soon as he reached home, and then closed the door and fastened it. All the neighbors were inside waiting for the feast of guavas, and as soon as the basket was opened they began to fight to get out of the windows. After a while Juan opened the door and when he saw his parents' swollen faces, he cried out, "What rich fine guavas those must have been! They have made you both so very fat."

Juan Makes Gulay of his own Child.

After Juan was married about a year a baby was born, and he and his wife loved it very much. But Juan was always obedient to his wife, being a fool, and when she told him to make gulay or stew he inquired of her of what he should make it. She replied of anac, meaning anac hang gabi. Then she went away for a while, and when she returned Juan had the gulay ready. She asked for the baby and was horrified to learn that Juan had made a stew of his own child, having taken her words literally.

Juan Wins a Wager for the Governor.

Juan was well known for a brave man, though a fool, and the priest and the governor wished to try him on a wager. The governor told him that the priest was dead, and ordered him to watch the body in the church that night. The priest lay down on the bier before the altar, and after Juan came the priest arose. Juan pushed him down again and ran out of the church and secured a club. Returning, he said to the priest, "You are dead; try to get up again and I will break you to pieces." So Juan proved himself to be a brave man, and the governor won his wager.

Juan Hides the Salt.

Juan's father came into possession of a sack of salt, which used to be very precious and an expensive commodity. He wished it hidden in a secure place and so told Juan to hide it till they should need it. Juan went out and after hunting for a long time hid it in a carabao wallow, and of course when they went to fetch it again nothing was left but the sack.

The Man in the Shroud.

Juan, being a joker, once thought to have a little fun at others' expense, so he robed himself in a shroud, placed a bier by the roadside, set candles around it, and lay down so that all who went by should see him and be frightened. A band of robbers went by that way, and seeing the corpse, besought it to give them luck. As it happened, they were more than usually fortunate, and when they returned they began to make offerings to him to secure continuance of their good fortune. As the entire proceeds of their adventures were held in common, they soon began to quarrel over the offerings to be made. The captain became angry, and drew his sword with a threat to run the corpse through for causing so much dissension among his men.

This frightened the sham dead man to such a degree that he jumped up and ran away, and the robbers, who were even more frightened than he, ran the other way, leaving all their plunder.

Juan then returned and gathered all the money and valuables left behind by the robbers, and carried them home. Now he had a friend who was very curious to know how he came into possession of so much wealth, and so Juan told him, only he said nothing about robbers, but told his friend, whose name was Pedro, that the things were the direct reward of God for his piety.

Pedro, being afraid of the woods, decided to lie just inside the church door; besides, that being a more sacred place, he felt sure that God would favor him even more than Juan. He arranged his bier with the candles around him, and lay down to await the shower of money that should reward his devotions. When the sacristan went to the church to ring the bell for vespers, he saw the body lying there, and not knowing of any corpse having been carried in, he was frightened and ran to tell the padre. The padre, when he had seen the body, said it was a miracle, and that it must be buried within the church, for the sanctification of the edifice.

But Pedro, now thoroughly frightened, jumped off the bier and ran away, and the priest and the sacristan ran the other way, so the poor man never received the reward for his piety, and the church was deprived of a new patron saint.

The Adventures of Juan.

Juan was lazy, Juan was a fool, and his mother never tired of scolding him and emphasizing her words by a beating. When Juan went to school he made more noise at his study than anybody else, but his reading was only gibberish.

His mother sent him to town to buy meat to eat with the boiled rice, and he bought a live crab which he set down in the road and told to go to his mother and be cooked for dinner. The crab promised, but as soon as Juan's back was turned ran in the other direction.

Juan went home after a while and asked for the crab, but there was none, and they ate their rice without ulam. His mother then went herself and left Juan to care for the baby. The baby cried and Juan examined it to find the cause, and found the soft spot on its head. "Aha! It has a boil. No wonder it cries!" And he stuck a knife into the soft spot, and the baby stopped crying. When his mother came back, Juan told her about the boil and that the baby was now asleep, but the mother said it was dead, and she beat Juan again.

Then she told Juan that if he could do nothing else he could at least cut firewood, so she gave him a bolo and sent him to the woods.

He found what looked to him like a good tree and prepared to cut it, but the tree was a magic tree and said to Juan, "Do not cut me and I will give you a goat that shakes silver money from its whiskers." Juan agreed, and the bark of the tree opened and the goat came out, and when Juan told him to shake his whiskers, money dropped out. Juan was very glad, for at last he had something he would not be beaten for. On his way home he met a friend, and told him of his good fortune. The man made him dead drunk and substituted another goat which had not the ability to shake money from its whiskers, and when the new goat was tried at home poor Juan was beaten and scolded.

Back he went to the tree, which he threatened to cut down for lying to him, but the tree said, "No, do not kill me and I will give you a magic net which you may cast even on dry ground or into a tree-top and it will return full of fish," and the tree did even so.

Again he met the friend, again he drank tuba until he was dead drunk, and again a worthless thing was substituted, and on reaching home he was beaten and scolded.

Once more Juan went to the magic tree, and this time he received a magic pot, always full of rice; and spoons always full of whatever ulam might be wished, and these went the way of the other gifts, to the false friend.

The fourth time he asked of the tree he was given a magic stick that would without hands beat and kill anything that the owner wished. "Only say to it 'Boombye, boomba,' and it will obey your word," said the tree.

When Juan met the false friend again, the false friend asked him what gift he had this time. "It is only a stick that if I say, 'Boombye, boomba,' will beat you to death," said Juan, and with that the stick leaped from his hand and began to belabor the wicked man. "Lintic na cahoy ito ay! Stop it and I will give you everything I stole from you." Juan ordered the stick to stop, but made the man, bruised and sore, carry the net, the pot, and the spoons, and lead the goat to Juan's home. There the goat shook silver from his beard till Juan's three brothers and his mother had all they could carry, and they dined from the pot and the magic spoons until they were full to their mouths.

"Now," said Juan, "you have beaten me and called me a fool all my life, but you are not ashamed to take good things when I get them. I will show you something else. Boombye, boomba!" and the stick began to beat them all. Quickly they agreed that Juan was head of the house, and he ordered the beating to stop.

Juan now became rich and respected, but he never trusted himself far from his stick day or night. One night a hundred robbers came to break into the house, to take all his goods, and kill him, but he said to the stick, "Boombye, boomba!" and with the swiftness of lightning the stick flew around, and all those struck fell dead till there was not one left. Juan was never troubled again by robbers, and in the end married a princess and lived happily ever after.

The Aderna Bird.

There was once a king who greatly desired to obtain an aderna bird, which is possessed of magical powers, has a wonderful song, and talks like men. This king had a beautiful daughter, and he promised her to any one who would bring him an aderna bird. Now the quest for the aderna bird is very dangerous, because, if the heart is not pure, the man who touches the bird becomes stone, and the bird escapes.

There were in that country three brothers, Juan, Diego, and Pedro, and they all agreed to set out together to catch the aderna bird. Afar in the mountains they saw him, and Diego, being the eldest, had first chance, and he caught the aderna bird, but being of impure life he became a stone, and the bird flew away over the mountains.

Juan and Pedro pursued it over the rocky way till at last they saw it again, and Pedro, being the next eldest, essayed to catch it. He, too, being a bad man, was turned into stone and the aderna bird flew over another mountain, and Juan, undaunted, followed alone.

When at last he saw the aderna bird he made a trap with a mirror with a snare in front and soon caught the bird. He made a cage for it and started on his homeward journey. When he reached the stone which was his brother Pedro, he begged the bird to undo its work and make him a man again, and the bird did so. Then the two went on to where Diego was, and again Juan entreated the bird to set the other brother free, and the bird did so.

But Pedro and Diego, far from being grateful for what Juan had done for them, bound him, choked him, beat him, and left him for dead far from any road or any habitation, and went on their way to the king with the aderna bird, expecting for one the hand of the princess and for the other a rich reward.

But the aderna bird would not sing. Said the king, "O Aderna Bird, why do you not sing?" The bird replied, "O Mighty King, I sing only for him who caught me." "Did these men catch you?" "No, O King, Juan caught me, and these men have beaten him and stolen me from him." So the king had them punished, and waited for the coming of Juan.

Juan meanwhile had freed himself from his bonds, and wandered sore and hungry and lame through the forest. At last he met an old man who said to him, "Juan, why do you not go to the king's house, for there they want you very much?" "Alas," said Juan, "I am not able to walk so far from weakness, and I fear I shall die here in the forest." "Do not fear," said the old man, "I have here a wonderful hat that, should you but whisper to it where you wish to go, in a moment you are transported there through the air."

So the old man gave him the hat, and Juan put it on and said, "Hat, if this be thy nature, carry me across the mountains to the king's palace." And the hat carried him immediately into the presence of the king. Then the aderna bird began to sing, and after a time Juan married the princess, and all went well for the rest of their lives.

The Story of Juan and the Monkey.

Juan was a farmer, a farmer so poor that he had only one shirt and one pair of trousers. Juan was much annoyed by monkeys, who stole his corn. So he set a trap and caught several of them. These he killed with a club until he came to the last, which said to him, "Juan, don't kill me and I will be your servant all your life." "But I will," said Juan. "You are a thief and do not deserve to live." "Juan, let me live, and I will bring you good fortune, and if you kill me you will be poor all your life." The monkey talked so eloquently that Juan let himself be persuaded, and took the monkey home with him. The monkey was true to his word, and served Juan faithfully, cooking, washing, and hunting food for him, and at night going to distant fields and stealing maize and palay which he added to Juan's little store.

One day the monkey said to Juan, "Juan, why do you not marry?" Said Juan, "How can I marry? I have nothing to keep a wife." "Take my advice," said the monkey, "and you can marry the king's daughter." Juan took the monkey's advice and they set out for the king's palace. Juan remained behind while the monkey went up to the palace alone. Outside he called, as the custom is, "Honorable people!" and the king said, "Come in." The king said, "Monkey, where do you walk?" and the monkey said, "Mr. King, I wish to borrow your salop. My master wishes to measure his money." The king lent him the salop (a measure of about two quarts), and the monkey returned to Juan. After a few hours he returned it with a large copper piece cunningly stuck to the bottom with paste. The king saw it and called the monkey's attention to it, but the monkey haughtily waved his hand, and told the king that a single coin was of no consequence to his master.

The next day he borrowed the salop again and the coin stuck in the bottom was half a peso, and the third day the coin was a peso, but these he assured the king were of no more consequence to his master than the copper. Then the king told the monkey to bring his master to call, and the monkey promised that after a few days he would.

They went home, and as Juan's clothes must be washed, Juan went to bed while the monkey washed and starched them, pulling, pressing, and smoothing them with his hands because he had no iron.

Then they went to call on the king, and the king told Juan that he should marry the princess as soon as he could show the king a large house, with a hundred head of cattle, carabao, horses, sheep, and goats. Juan was very despondent at this, though he was too brave to let the king know his thoughts, he told his troubles to the monkey, who assured him that the matter was very easy.

The next day they took a drum and a shovel and went into the mountains, where there was a great enchanter who was a very wealthy man and also an asuang. They dug a great hole and then Juan hid in the woods and began to beat his drum, and the monkey rushed up to the enchanter's house and told him the soldiers were coming, and that he would hide him. So the enchanter went with the monkey to the hole and the monkey pushed him in and began with hands and feet to cover him up. Juan helped, and soon the enchanter was dead and buried. Then they went to the house and at the first door they opened they liberated fifty people who were being fattened for the enchanter's table. These people were glad to help Juan convey all the money, cattle, and all the enchanter's wealth to the town. Juan built a house on the plaza, married the princess, and lived happily ever after, but his friend the monkey, having so well earned his liberty, he sent back to the woods, and their friendship still continued.

Juan the Drunkard who Visited Heaven.

There was once a man named Juan, who was a drunkard. One day when he was drunker than usual he decided to visit his dead friends in heaven. He took no baggage except two long bamboo buckets full of tuba, which he carried one over each shoulder. He walked and walked for at least a week, until he came to a place where they sold tuba. There he filled his buckets, promising to pay on his return, and set out again.

After walking a long time he came to a city with a wall around it, and at the gate sat an old man with a long beard and with keys at his girdle whom he knew at once as St. Peter. "Good-morning, St. Peter," said Juan. "I would like to see some of my friends that I think are here." "Who are you?" asked St. Peter, getting up angrily. "I am Juan and I have come a long way to see some of my friends. Won't you let me look?" "No," said St. Peter, "I won't. You are drunk." "Well, then, only be so good as to let me take just a little peep." So St. Peter opened the gate just the least bit, but Juan was not satisfied, so he said, "Good St. Peter, open the gate just a little wider for me to see with both eyes." Then he persuaded St. Peter to let him put his head in, and then by a little firmness he slipped in, still carrying his buckets of tuba.

St. Peter ordered him to come out, but he started down a street he saw, or rather a road, for there were no houses there. "Stop!" said St. Peter, "that road won't take you to your friends. Go the other way." And Juan did so.

After he had gone on for some time, he found that he was surrounded by devils who began to torment him, but he defended himself succesfully against them, and by giving them part of his tuba bribed them to tell him where to find his friends. To his friends he gave the remainder of his tuba and then set out to find God himself.

Being ushered into the Divine Presence, he knelt humbly and said, "Lord, I beg thee to tell me how long I shall live." The Lord looked at him and said, "I have not sent for you; why are you here?" Juan bowed more humbly than before, and replied, "O Most High, I have come to see some of my dead friends, and I would like also to know how long I shall live on earth." So God told him that he had still a long earthly life before him and never to come again until he was sent for.

So Juan left the heavenly city and passed back through St. Peter's gate, and at last, after a weary journey, came to earth again. And Juan lived a long and happy life and drank more tuba than ever.

The Juan who Visited Heaven.

There was once an old couple who always prayed for a child, for they had always been childless. No matter how it looked, whether deformed or ugly, they must have a child. So after a short time they saw that their prayers would be answered, and in the course of nature a child was born, but the mother died at the birth.

The new-born child ran to the church, climbed into the tower, and began to hammer on the bells. The priest, hearing the noise, sent the sacristan to see what was the matter. The sacristan went, and seeing there a little child, asked what he was doing and told him to stop, for the priest would be angry; but the ringing of the bells went on. Then the priest went up. "Little boy," he said, "what is your name?" "Juan," said the child. "Why are you ringing the church bells?" "Because my mother is dead." "When did she die?" "Only now." "If you stop ringing the bells she shall have a fine funeral and you shall live with me and be as my son," said the priest. "Very well, sir, if you will let me stay in the church all I wish." To this the priest assented. The dead woman was buried with all the pomp of music, candles, and bells, and the boy went to live in the convent. Always after his school was done he would be in the church. The father did everything that was possible for him, for he knew that he was not a natural child.

After a time the padre sent for him to get his dinner, but he would not leave the church, so the priest had a good dinner cooked and sent it down to the church, but he told the sacristan to watch the church and see what happened. The sacristan watched and soon saw the statue of Jesus eating with the boy. This he told the padre, and the child's dinner was always sent to the church after that. One day not long after he went to the priest and said, "Master, my friend down at the church wants me to go away with him." "Where are you going?" "My friend wants me to go to heaven with him."

The priest consented and the little boy and the Lord Jesus went away together. As they walked the little boy saw that two roads ran along together, one thorny and the other smooth. Asked the boy of his companion, "Friend, why is this road where we walk so thorny, and that other yonder so smooth?" Said the Lord, "Hush, child, it is not fitting to disturb the peace of this place, but I will tell you. This is the path of the sinless and is thorny, but that smooth way yonder is the way of the sinners and never reaches heaven."

Again they came to a great house filled with young men and women who were all working hammering iron. Said the little boy, "Who are those who labor with the hammer?" "Hush, child, they are the souls of those who died unmarried."

They journeyed on, and on one side were bush pastures filled with poor cattle while on the opposite side of the road were pastures dry and bare where the cattle were very fat. The child inquired the meaning of the mystery. The Lord answered him, "Hush, child! These lean cattle in the rich pastures are the souls of sinners, while those fat cattle on dry and sunburnt ground are the souls of sinless ones."

After a while they crossed a river, one part of which was ruby red and the other spotless white. "Friend, what is this?" asked the boy. "Hush, child, the red is the blood of your mother whose life was given for yours, and the white is the milk which she desired to give to you, her child," said the Lord.

At last they came to a great house having seven stories, and there on a table they saw many candles, some long, some short, some burned out. Said Juan, "Friend, what are all these candles?" "Hush, child, those are the lives of your friends." "What are those empty candlesticks?" "Those are your mother and your uncle, who are dead." "Who is this long one?" "That is your father, who has long to live." "Who is this very short one?" "That is your master, who will die soon." "May I put in another?" "Yes, child, if you wish." So he changed it for a long one, and with his heavenly companion he returned to earth.

There he told his master, the padre, all that he had seen and heard and how he had changed the candles; and he and his master lived together a very long time. And in the fulness of time the padre died, but Juan went to heaven one day with his Lord and never returned.

The Sad Story of Juan and Maria.

Juan and Maria were orphans. When Juan was about eight years old and Maria was about four their father died. The mother went into the hemp fields to earn a living for her family by stripping the fibre from the hemp, which is very hard work, so hard that she died worn out in a month or two afterward.

Juan and Maria were then taken into the family of an uncle, their mother's brother, and little Juan began to work for his little sister's and his own living, by transplanting the tender shoots of the banana. Maria often accompanied him, as the children were much attached to each other. One day when they were out in the field Maria saw a beautiful bird which seemed very tame and tried to catch it, but the bird ran into the woods, and although she could come very close to it she could not catch it. On and on she went until she was almost ready to drop, her tiny feet leaving no trace, but still she followed the bird. Just at night she saw an old man with a very kind face, who came toward her, and putting the bird under one arm and taking Maria on his shoulder, he set off toward his house, which did not seem to be very far off. Arriving there he said to his wife, "See, wife, what good fortune I have had today." Seeing the child, his wife threw up her hands in thanksgiving and cried, "Thanks be to God, we have a child at last in our old age."

Poor Juan, torn with fear, hunted the woods for days, but could not find his little sister. Convinced at last that his search was hopeless, he went home and worked hard and in a few years became a rich man. Then he began to consider where he could find a suitable wife. It was told him that there was an old couple beyond three ranges of mountains who had a beautiful daughter, and to her he determined to go.

Maria had likewise grown up, and now she was the most beautiful damsel in many days' journey. When Juan set out on his search, it was to the house of Maria's foster parents that he was bound.

Arriving there, he called to those within, "Honorable people," and the old man said, "Come in;" but Juan remained without until the third invitation. Passing within, he likewise would not sit down till he had been asked three times.

Seating himself on a bench, he told the old man that he had come to marry his daughter, and the old man told him he might if he could show that he had enough money. As Juan was rich, this did not take long to do, and after a few days Juan and Maria were married, not knowing their relationship. They lived happily together, and a daughter was born to them. This child, like her mother, was very beautiful.

One day, as the little girl was playing by the river, a crab came to the edge of the water and said,—

"Beautiful art thou,

More beautiful than any other,

But thou art the child

Of sister and brother."

Horrified, the child ran to her mother, and then the parents began to talk over the events of their childhood and found that they were indeed sister and brother.

They went to Maria's foster father to ask what they must do, and he told them they must live apart; and then they went to the archbishop, who told them that they might live lawfully together, as the sacrament of marriage was above all, but, after much thought, they decided that they must live apart, and Maria went back to her foster father.

Thus by a sinless crime were their lives saddened forever.

The Fifty-one Thieves.

There were once two brothers, Juan and Pedro. Pedro was rich and was the elder, but Juan was very poor and gained his living by cutting wood. Juan became so poor at last that he was forced to ask alms from his brother, or what was only the same thing, a loan. After much pleading, Pedro gave his brother enough rice for a single meal, but repenting of such generosity, went and took it off the fire, as his brother's wife was cooking it, and carried it home again.

Juan then set out for the woods, thinking he might be able to find a few sticks that he could exchange for something to eat, and went much farther than he was accustomed to go. He came to a road he did not know and followed it for some distance to where it led to a great rocky bluff and there came to an end.

Juan did not know exactly what to think of such an abrupt ending to the roadway, and sat down behind a large rock to meditate. As he sat there a voice within the cliff said, "Open the door," and a door in the cliff opened itself. A man richly dressed came out, followed by several others, whom he told that they were going to a town at a considerable distance. He then said, "Shut the door," and the door closed itself again.

Juan was not sure whether any one else was inside, but he was no coward and besides he thought he might as well be murdered as starved to death, so when the robbers had ridden away to a safe distance without seeing him, he went boldly up to the cliff and said, "Open the door." The door opened as obediently to him as to the robber, and he went in. He found himself inside a great cavern filled with money, jewels, and rich stuffs of every kind.

Hastily gathering more than enough gold and jewels to make him rich, he went outside, not forgetting to say, "Close the door," and went back to his house.

Having hidden all but a little of his new wealth, he wished to change one or two of his gold pieces for silver so that he could buy something to eat. He went to his brother's house to ask him for the favor, but Pedro was not at home, and his wife, who was at least as mean as Pedro, would not change the money. After a while Pedro came home, and his wife told him that Juan had some money; and Pedro, hoping in turn to gain some advantage, went to Juan's house and asked many questions about the money. Juan told him that he had sold some wood in town and had been paid in gold, but Pedro did not believe him and hid himself under the house to listen. At night he heard Juan talking to his wife, and found out the place and the password. Immediately taking three horses to carry his spoils, he set out for the robbers' cave.

Once arrived, he went straight to the cliff and said, "Open the door," and the door opened immediately. He went inside and said, "Close the door," and the door closed tight. He gathered together fifteen great bags of money, each all he could lift, and carried them to the door ready to put on the horses. He found all the rich food and wine of the robbers in the cave, and could not resist the temptation to make merry at their expense; so he ate their food and drank their fine wines till he was foolishly drunk. When he had reached this state, he began to think of returning home. Beating on the door with both hands, he cried out, "Open, beast. Open, fool. May lightning blast you if you do not open!" and a hundred other foolish things, but never once saying, "Open the door."

While he was thus engaged, the robbers returned, and hearing them coming he hid under a great pile of money with only his nose sticking out. The robbers saw that some one had visited the cave in their absence and hunted for the intruder till one of them discovered him trembling under a heap of coin. With a shout they hauled him forth and beat him until his flesh hung in ribbons. Then they split him into halves and threw the body into the river, and cut his horses into bits, which they threw after him.

When Pedro did not return, his wife became anxious and told Juan where he had gone. Juan stole quietly to the place by night, and recovered the body, carried it home, and had the pieces sewn together by the tailor.

Now the robbers knew that they had been robbed by some one else, and so, when Pedro's body was taken away, the captain went to town to see who had buried the body, and by inquiring, found that Juan had become suddenly rich, and also that it was his brother who had been buried.

So the captain of the robbers went to Juan's house, where he found a ball going on. Juan knew the captain again and that he was asking many questions, so he made the captain welcome and gave him a great deal to eat and drink. One of the servants came in and pretended to admire the captain's sword till he got it into his own hands; and then he began to give an exhibition of fencing, making the sword whirl hither and thither and ending with a wonderful stroke that made the captain's head roll on the floor.

A day or two later, the lieutenant also came to town, and began to make inquiries concerning the captain. He soon found out that the captain had been killed in Juan's house, but Juan now had soldiers on guard at his door, so that it was necessary to use strategy. He went to Juan and asked if he could start a "tienda," or wine-shop, and Juan, who recognized the lieutenant, said, "Yes." Then the lieutenant went away, soon returning with seven great casks, in each of which he had seven men.

These he stored under Juan's house until such time as Juan, being asleep, could be killed with certainty and little danger. When this was done, he went into the house, intending to make Juan drunk and then kill him as Juan had the captain. Juan, however, got the lieutenant drunk first, and soon his head, like the captain's, rolled on the floor.

The soldiers below, like all soldiers, wished to have a drink from the great casks, and so one of them took a borer and bored into one of the casks. As he did so, a voice whispered, "Is Juan asleep yet?" The soldier replied, "Not yet," and went and told Juan. The casks by his order were all put into a boat, loaded with stones and chains, and thrown into the sea. So perished the last of the robbers.

Juan, being no longer in fear of the robbers, often went to their cave, and helped himself to everything that he wanted. He finally became a very great and wealthy man.

The Covetous King and the Three Children.

There were once three orphan children, the oldest of whom was perhaps ten years old, and the others but little things, almost babies. They had a tiny little tumble-down house to live in, but very little to eat. Said the eldest to his little brother and sister, "I will go yonder on the sands laid bare by the falling tide, and it may be that I shall find something that we can eat." The little children begged to go, too, and they all set out over the sands. Soon they found a large living shell. "Thanks be to God," said the boy, for he was well instructed, "we shall have something to eat." "Take me home, but do not cook me," said the shell, "and I will work for you." Now this was probably the Holy Virgin herself, in the form of a shell, who had taken pity on the poor children. They took the shell home, and there it spoke again. "Put me into the rice pot, cover me up, and you shall turn out plenty of boiled rice for all of you." And they did so, and the boiled rice came from the pot. "Now put me into the other pot, and take out ulam." And they took out ulam in abundance. "Have you a clothes chest?" asked the shell; but there was none, so they put it into a box, and the box became filled with clothing. Then the shell filled the spare room with rice, and last of all filled another large box with money.

Now the king of this city was a cruel man, and he sent for the children and told them that they must give up their money, their rice and all to him and be poor again. "O dear king," said the oldest child, "will you not leave us a little for our living?" "No," replied the king, "I will give you as much boiled rice as you need, and you ought to be glad that you get it."

So the king sent ten soldiers to move the rice and the money, but, as soon as they got it to the king's house, it returned to the children. The soldiers worked a whole week without getting a grain of rice or a piece of money to stay in the king's house. Then because they were about to die from fatigue, the king sent ten more, and these too failed. Then the king went himself, but when he tried to move the money he fell down dead. The children, relieved from persecution, lived long and happy lives and were always rich and influential people.

The Silent Lover.

A long time ago, when the world was young, there lived a very bashful young man. Not far from his house there lived the most beautiful young woman in the world. The young woman had many suitors but rejected all, wishing only for the love of the bashful young man. He in his turn was accustomed to follow her about, longing for courage to declare his love, but bashfulness always sealed his lips. At last, despairing of ever making his unruly tongue tell of his passion, he took a dagger and, following her to the bathing place on the river bank, he cut out his own heart, cast it at her feet, and fell down lifeless. The girl fled, terrified, and a crow pounced upon the heart, and carried it to a hollow dao-tree, when it fell from his beak into the hollow and there remained. But the love for the girl was so strong in the heart that it became reanimated and clothed again with humanity in the form of a little child. A hunter, pursuing the wild boar with dogs, found the child crying from hunger at the foot of the dao-tree and, being childless, took it home, and he and his old wife cared for it as their own. The young woman, knowing now the love of the young man, lived for his memory's sake, a widow, rejecting all suitors.

But from the child was never absent the image of his loved one, and at last his love so wrought on his weak frame that he sickened. Knowing that his end was near, he begged of his foster mother that, after his death, she should leave him, and not be surprised if she could not find him on her return. He also asked that on the third day she should take whatever she should find in a certain compartment of the great chest and give it to the girl without price. All this she promised, realizing fully that this was not a natural child.

At last he died, and when his foster mother left the body, his great love reanimated the body and it crept into the chest, becoming there transformed into a beautifully carved casket of fragrant wood.

Obedient to his wishes, on the third day the old woman carried the casket to the girl, giving it to her without price.

When the girl took the casket into her hands, its charm fascinated her, and she clasped it tight and covered it with kisses. At last the spell was broken by the magic of her kisses, and the casket whispered softly to her, "I am thy true love. I was the heart of him who killed himself for love of thee, and I was the youth who died for love of thee, but at last I am contented. In life and death we shall never more be separated." And it was so, for the woman lived to a great age, carrying the casket always with her, inhaling its fragrance with her kisses, and when she died it was buried with her.

The Priest, the Servant Boy, and the Child Jesus.

There was once a priest who had for his servant a very good boy. One day the padre wanted the boy, and, after looking everywhere for him, went to church. Opening the door quietly, he looked in and there he saw that the statue of the child Jesus had left its shrine and was down on the floor talking and playing with the boy. The priest slipped softly away and ordered a very fine dinner cooked for the lad. When the boy returned to the convent, the padre asked him where he had been. "I have been down to the church playing with a friend." "Very well, there is your dinner. If you play with your friend again, ask him if I shall go to glory in heaven when I am dead." The boy took his dinner to the church and ate, sharing it With the child Jesus.

"Tell me, friend," said he to his heavenly companion, "will my master, the priest, go to glory in heaven?"

"No," said the child Jesus, "because he has neglected his father and mother." When the boy carried these words to the priest he became very sad, and asked the lad to inquire whether he might atone for his wrong by doing good to other old people. "No," came the answer. "It must be his father and mother who shall receive their dues, and it may be that he shall enter heaven alive."

So the priest sent for his poor old father and mother, and lavished on them every care, suffering no one else to do the least thing for them. At last the old people died, and the priest was very sad. Then one night, as he slept, came soft and very beautiful music around about and within the convent, and the boy awoke the priest to listen. "Oh," said the padre, "it is perhaps the angels come to carry us alive to heaven." And it was so. The angels carried the boy and the priest, his master, to be in glory in heaven.

The Story of Juan del Mundo de Austria and the Princess Maria.

There was once a king who had three very beautiful daughters, Princess

Clara, Princess Catalina, and Princess Maria.

This king was sick for a long time with a dreadful disease, and although he spent much money on medicines and doctors he was only worse instead of better.

At last he sent word to all his people proclaiming that whoever would cure him might have one of the princesses to marry.

After several days one of the heralds returned, saying he had met a snake who inquired if the king would give his daughter to a snake to wife if he were cured. The king called his daughters and asked if they would be willing to marry a snake.

Said Princess Clara, "I will be stung by a snake till I am dead before I give my virginity to a snake." Said Princess Catalina, "I may be beaten to death with sticks, but I will not give my virginity to a snake." Said Princess Maria, "Father, so you be but well, I care not what becomes of me. If a snake can cure you, I am willing to marry him."

So the king's message was carried to the snake, and the king was made well. The snake and the princess were married, and set off through the forest together. After a long journey they came to a house in the forest, and there the snake and the beautiful Maria lived together many days. But the snake, being very wise, saw that the princess ate little and cried very much, and asked her why it was so. She told him that it was hard for her to live with a snake. "Very well," said the snake, and went into a house near by; after a little there came out a handsome man with silken clothes, and rings on his fingers, who told her that he was her husband, that he was known among men as Don Juan del Mundo de Austria, and that he was king of all the beasts, being able to take the form of any of them at will.

They passed many happy days together till the time came for the great feast at the court of Princess Maria's father. Don Juan told her that she might go, but that she must on no account tell his name or rank, otherwise when she came to their trysting-place by the seashore she would not find him. He gave her a magic ring by means of which she might obtain anything she wanted, and left her close to her own city.

When she arrived at home her sisters were greatly surprised to see her looking well, happy, and much more finely dressed than when she went away, but her father was very glad to see her. The elder sisters often asked her the secret of her husband's identity, but her answer was always the same, "Did you not both see that I married a snake? Who else could it be." The wicked women then determined to make her tell, whether she wished or not, and so they asked her to walk with them in a secluded garden.

Then they took sticks and set upon her, beating her and telling her that she must tell who her husband was. The poor little princess defended herself a long time, saying that if she told she would never see him again, but finally, when she was nearly dead from beating, she told them that her husband was Don Juan de Austria. Then she was beaten for not telling the truth, but her tormentors finally desisted and she went to her father and told him all.

He did not wish her to return to the forest and begged her to remain with him, but she insisted.

When she arrived at the trysting-place, Don Juan was not there, but she set out bravely, asking of her ring whatever she needed for food, drink, and clothing. Wherever she went she inquired of the beasts and birds the whereabouts of her husband, Don Juan de Austria, and, when they knew who she was, they worshipped her and did all that was required.

After many days of wandering she came to a place where there was a giant, who was about to eat her, but when he knew her for Don Juan's wife he worshipped her and sent her on her way. Soon she was found by a young giantess who, too, was about to eat her, but when she learned that Maria was the wife of Don Juan she carried her to her own house and hid her, saying that she must be cared for a while until her parents should return, for they might eat her without asking who she was. When the old giant and his wife came back, they told her that she must stay with them for a while, until they could find out about the whereabouts of Don Juan, when they would help her further.

They were very good to her, for, said they, "Don Juan is not only king of the animals but of the giants and monsters of every kind."

Then the giants took her to Don Juan's city and found her a place in the house of an old childless couple, and there she made her home. But Don Juan had taken another wife, the Lady Loriana, and the new wife saw the old and desired her for a servant. So the Princess Maria became a servant of her rival, and often sat in old rags under the stairs at her work, while her faithless husband passed her without seeing her.

The poor girl was torn with jealousy and spent much time thinking about how she might win her husband again. So she asked the ring for a toy in the form of a beautiful little chick, just from the egg.

The Lady Loriana saw the pretty toy and begged for it. "No," said Maria, "unless you grant me a little favor, that I may sleep on the floor to-night in your room." So Loriana, suspecting no deceit, agreed.

That night Maria wished on her ring that Loriana might be overcome with sleep, and again that her own rags might be transformed into royal raiment and that her tiara should glitter on her forehead. Then she went to the head of the bed and called Don Juan. At first he would not answer, then, without turning to look at the speaker, he bade her go away, as his wife would be angry. "But that is not your wife, Don Juan," said Maria; "I am your true wife, Maria. Look at my dress and the jewels on my forehead—my face, the ring on my finger." And Don Juan saw that she was indeed the deserted wife, and after he had heard the sad story of her wanderings he loved her afresh. The next day at noon-time Maria was not to be found, although Dona Loriana looked everywhere. At last she looked into Don Juan's room, and there, locked in each other's arms fast asleep, were Don Juan and Princess Maria.

Loriana aroused them, angrily saying to Maria, "Why do you wish to steal my husband? You must leave this house at once." But Maria resisted saying, "No, he is not your husband but mine, and I will not give him up." And so they quarrelled long and bitterly, but at last agreed to be judged by the council.

There each told her story, and Maria showed Don Juan's enchanted ring, which worked its wonders for her but would not obey the Lady Loriana.

When the matter was decided, it was the judgment of all, including the Archbishop, that Maria was the lawful wife, but that she and Don Juan must go away and never return.

So Don Juan and the Princess Maria went away and lived long and happily.

The Artificial Earthquake.

There was once in another town a man who had three daughters, all very beautiful. But one of them had an admirer, who by some means excited the old man's wrath, and the daughter was sent to a distant place.

This in turn made the young man angry, and he determined to have revenge. He took a strong rope and attached it to one of the corner upright posts of the house, and waiting till it was dark and still inside, he hid behind a tree and began to pull the rope, alternately hauling and slacking.

"Oh!" said one of the girls, "there is an earthquake."

The old man jumped up and, seizing his crucifix, began to recite the prayers against earthquakes. But the trembling kept up. For more than an hour the old man prayed to all the saints in the calendar, but the earthquake still shook the house.

Then the earthquake stopped a moment, and a voice called him to come outside. His daughters begged him not to go, for said they, "You never can stand such a terrible earthquake." Taking his saw, his axe, and his long bolo, the old man went down, only to find everything quiet outside. He began to explore the surroundings of the house to see if he could find the cause of the disturbance, and fell over the rope. With that he began to curse and swear, saying, "May lightning blast the one of ill-omened ancestry who has shaken my house, frightened my family, and broken my bones," and many other harsh things, but he got no answer but a laugh, and the young man had his revenge.

The Queen and the Aeta Woman.

There was once a king who was sick unto death. Though he was already married to a beautiful and charming woman, he promised to marry any woman who could save his life or recall him after death. Then he died and after his death the queen was superintending the preparations for burial and getting ready the collation for the mourners. While she was busy, an Aeta (Negrito) woman, black, ill-favored, dirty, and smelling like a goat went into the room. Kneeling by the body, she began pulling out pins from the flesh, and soon the king awoke, but his mind was lost. He clasped the Aeta woman to him and showered on her terms of endearment, thinking that she was the queen, while all the time the real queen was without.

Seeing how matters stood, the Aeta woman called the queen, "Maria, Maria, bring food for the king," and she forced the queen to obey her and work as a slave in the kitchen, while she wore the queen's robes and lay on the queen's couch. Of course this made a scandal, but no one could interfere until at last a soldier passed through the kitchen and seeing the queen's face red with the fire and noting her beauty, he called the king's attention to her. Then the king remembered Maria and that she was the real queen, and that the other was only a hideous Aeta usurper, and he had the Aeta woman tied in a sack with stones and thrown into the sea.

The Child Saint.

Once there was a child who was different from other children. She was very quiet and patient, and never spoke unless she was spoken to. Her mother used to urge her to play in the streets with the other children, but she always preferred to sit in the corner quietly and without trouble to any one. When the time came for the child to enter school, she begged her mother to get her a book of doctrines and let her learn at home. So her mother got a book of doctrines for her, and she was able to read at once without being taught. Day after day she sat in the corner reading her books and meditating.

When she became a little larger she asked to have a little room built away from the house, where she might remain free from the intrusion of any earthly thought.

Her mother had this done, and there in the tight little room with no one to see her she sat. She never tasted the food or drink placed at her door, and finally her mother, becoming alarmed, made a tiny hole and peeped through the wall. There sat the child reading her book, with a huge man standing beside her, and all manner of beasts and serpents filling the little room.

More frightened than ever, the mother ran to the priest, who told her that those were devils tempting the child, but not to fear, for she would certainly become a saint. And it was so, for afterwards the evil shapes were gone. Then the priest and the people built a costly shrine and placed her in it, and there the people used to go and ask her to intercede for them. But at last the shrine was found empty, and surely she was taken alive into heaven and is now a saint.

Tagalog Babes in the Woods.

Once upon a time there was a cruel father who hated his twin children,

Juan and Maria, and drove them from the house on every occasion.

The children used to live on the grains of rice that fell through the bamboo floor, and such food as their mother could smuggle to them.

At last, when they were about six years old, their father took them off into the forest and left them without food or drink. They wandered for three days, being preserved by such fruits and leaves as they could gather.

Finally poor Maria said she could go no farther, but that she would die. Juan cut a mountain bamboo and from its hollow joints gave Maria a refreshing drink. Then he climbed a tree and in the distance saw a house. After much exertion they reached it and called out, "Tauo po." A voice from within said, "Come in, children." They went in and found a table set, but no one was there, though the same voice said, "Eat and drink all you want." They did so, and after saying, "Thank you, good-by," they started to go away, but again they were bidden to stay. So they stayed on for a long time until Juan was a young man and Maria a young woman. From a great chest that stood in the corner they took out new clothing as their old wore out, and the chest was never empty, and there was always food in the magic dishes on the table.

The King, the Princess, and the Poor Boy.

There was once a king who loved his daughter very much, so much in fact that he did not wish her to marry; so he built for her a secret house or vault under the ground, and there he kept her away from all but her parents and her maid servants.

There was also an old man in the same city who had a son. The old man said to his son, "Come, lad, let us go into the country and plant crops that we may live," for they were very poor. After they had worked a short time in the country, the old man died and the boy returned to the king's city and then went up and down the street crying, "Oh! who will buy me for a slave, that I may bury my father?" A kind-hearted rich man saw him and inquired his troubles, and the boy told him that he was greatly grieved because his father was dead and he had no money for the funeral. The rich man told him not to grieve, that his father would be buried with all the ceremonies given to any one. After the funeral the boy went to live with the rich man as his servant, and served him faithfully; so faithfully, indeed, that the rich man, who was childless, adopted him and gave him every advantage of education.

One day the boy wrote a sentence and placed it in the window, "You may hide your treasure with every care, and watch it well, but it will be spent at last." Now the boy had no idea of any hidden meaning in this sentence, but the king chanced to pass that way and read it. Angrily he called the rich man to his carriage, and demanded of him what it meant. "I do not know, most exalted king," said the rich man, "I have only now seen it. It must have been written by a poor boy to whom I have given shelter since his father died." "Drive him away," said the king; "if he comes back he shall be put to death."

So the rich man with a heavy heart, for he loved the boy, sent him out into the world. The boy wandered far and long, till at last he came to a house. He called out to those within, "Honorable people," and heard them answer, "Come in." Inside there was no one but only two statues, and one of these spoke, bidding him return to his own town and beg of his master princely clothing, a princely carriage, all gilt, and a music box that could play many tunes.

So the poor boy returned to his master, who sent for the tradesmen and tailors and had them make all manner of princely clothing.

Then he got into his carriage and drove around for a while, till he met a boy. To the boy he gave the music box and a piece of money and told him to play it everywhere but to sell it to nobody, and to report to him if any one wanted it. So the boy got into the carriage and took the music box with him, while the poor boy went back to the rich man's house.

Soon the king saw the beautiful carriage and heard the sweet music of the music box. The king asked the boy who the owner was, and wished to buy them. The boy told the king that he must tell his employer, and soon the carriage and the music box were sent to the king for a present.

The king was much pleased, for he knew the princess would be delighted, so he had the carriage and the music box taken into her vault, and played on the music box a long time. After he had gone, out stepped the poor boy from a secret compartment of the carriage, and knelt before her telling his love in gentle tones. She listened to him, much frightened at first, but later more composedly, till at last she gave him her heart and promised him her hand.

When the king came in again he found them sitting holding each other's hands. He demanded in a loud voice, "Who are you? Why are you here? How did you come?" To this the boy modestly replied, saying that he had come concealed in the carriage, and told the king that "You may hide your treasure with every care, and watch it well, but it will be spent at last." But the princess entreated for him, and finally the king gave his consent to their marriage, and they lived happily ever after.

Hidden Treasure.

There were once a husband and his wife who were very poor. They had a little plot of ground that helped to sustain them, but as the man was sick the woman went to work alone.

As she was weeding in the fields she found a malapad, and after a little she found another, and so on until she had a sec-apat. With this she returned home and bought rice, but she was afraid to tell her husband lest he be jealous.

The next day she went to work and on this day she found a silver peso. As she reached the edge of the field a voice spoke to her saying, "Tell no one of your good fortune, not even your husband, and you shall have more treasure." Afterwards she went to the field, and daily she found a peso until she had five pesos, which she hid in a safe place.

On the seventh day she went to the field, but found nothing. She went to the edge of the field to boil her rice, and was blowing her fire when she heard the same voice again saying, "Never mind boiling your rice, but dig there under your pallok, and you will find more than enough. Tell no one, not even your husband, of what you find." She dug down and there she found a great jar filled to the brim with gold pieces. She took one or two, and hastily covered up the rest and went home. Like a good wife she disliked to keep a secret from her husband, and finally she took him off to a quiet place and told him of their good fortune.

He, overjoyed, could not restrain himself and went into the village and told every one of the treasure trove. Then they went to dig it up, but it was no longer there. Even the gold and the five pesos already saved and hid in another secret place were gone, and they were as poor as they had been before.

How foolish they were to disobey the command of the voice!

The Battle of the Enchanters.

There was once a poor boy who was very ambitious to learn, and with the consent of his parents he bound himself to an enchanter who was a very wise man. The boy remained with him for a very long time, until at last his master sent him home, saying that he could teach him nothing more. The boy went home, but there he found nothing in the way of adventure, so he proposed to his father that he should become a horse, which his father could sell for twenty pesos to his late teacher. He cautioned his father that, as soon as he received the money for the horse, he should drop the halter as if by accident.

The young man then became a horse, and his father took him to the enchanter, who gave him twenty pesos. As soon as the money was in the father's hand, he dropped the halter, and the horse at once became a bird which flew away. The enchanter metamorphosed himself into a hawk and followed.

The bird was so hard pressed by the hawk that it dived into the sea and became a fish. The hawk followed and became a shark. The fish, being in danger from the shark, leaped out on to the dry ground and took the shape of a crab, which hid in a spring where a princess was bathing. The shark followed in the shape of a cat, which began to search under the stones for the crab, but the crab escaped by changing itself into a ring on the finger of the princess.

Now it chanced that the father of the princess was very sick, and the enchanter went to the palace and offered to cure him for the ring on the finger of the princess. To this the king agreed, but the ring begged the princess not to give him directly to the enchanter, but to let him fall on the floor. The princess did this, and as the ring touched the floor it broke into a shower of rice. The enchanter immediately took the form of a cock and industriously pecked at the grains on the floor. But as he pecked, one of the grains changed to a cat which jumped on him and killed him.

The young man then resumed his own form, having proven himself a greater man than his master.

Fletcher Gardner.

Bloomington, Ind.

PART IV

A Filipino (Tagalog) Version of Aladdin.

Once on a time a poor boy and his mother went far from their home city to seek their fortune. They were very poor, for the husband and father had died, leaving them little, and that little was soon spent. The boy went into the market-place to seek for work, and a travelling merchant, seeing his distress, spoke to him and asked many questions. When he had inquired the name of the boy's father, he embraced him with many kind words, and told him that he was the father's long-lost brother, and that as he had no children of his own the boy should be his heir and for the present live with him as his son. He sent the boy to call his mother, and when she came he kissed her with many words of endearment, and would have it that she was his sister-in-law, though she told him that her husband had no brother. He treated her well and made her many presents, so that she was forced to believe he really was her brother-in-law.

The merchant then invited the boy to go for a visit with him, promising that the mother should soon follow. Mother and son consented, and the merchant set off with his nephew in the afternoon. They went far and came to a mountain which they crossed, and then to a second, which seemed very high to the poor boy so that he begged to rest. The man would not allow this, and when the boy cried, beat him till he agreed to do whatever he was told. They crossed this mountain also, and came to a third, and on the very top they stopped. The merchant drew a ring from his own finger and put it on that of the boy. Then he drew a circle around the boy and told him not to be frightened at what would happen, but to stretch out his arms three times, and that the third time the ground would open, and that then he must descend and get a tabo that he would find, and that with that in their hands they could quickly return. The boy, from fear of the man, did as he was told, and when the ground opened, went down into the cave and got the tabo. As he reached up his hand to be pulled from the cave, the man took the ring from his finger, and told him to hand up the vessel, but the boy, now much frightened, refused unless he were first helped out himself. That the man would not do, and after much talk drew another circle around the cave-mouth, bade it close, and left the boy a prisoner in most evil plight.

Alone and helpless for three days in the underground darkness, the boy was a prey to awful fear, but at the end of the third day, having by accident rubbed slightly the tabo with his hand, at once a great sinio or multo stood before him, saying that he was the slave of the tabo, and that all things earthly were within his power. At once mindful of his mother, he told the multo to take him home, and in the winking of an eye, still carrying the tabo in his hand, he stood before his mother. He found her very hungry and sorrowful, and recounted all that had happened and again rubbed the tabo lightly. The multo reappeared and the good woman hid her face for terror at the sight, but the lad bade the multo bring him a dinner for them both on a service of silver with everything to match.

After they had dined well for several days on the remnants of the food, the boy went to the market and sold the spoons that the multo had brought for two gold pieces, and on that they lived a long time: and as from time to time their money became exhausted, he sold more, till at last there was nothing left. Then, as he had become a young man, he required the multo to bring him a great chest of money, and soon became known as a very rich and generous person.

Now there was in that city a woman who had a very handsome daughter whom she wished to marry to the young man, and by way of opening the matter, she and her daughter went one day to try to buy some of the rich table ware which he had, or at least so they pretended. The young man was not of a mind for that kind of alliance, and so told the old woman to rub the magic vessel. She did so and the multo at once whisked her inside. The daughter also went in to inquire for her mother, and as she admiringly touched the tabo the multo made her prisoner, and the two became the slaves of the young man and were never heard of again.

A variant of this tale has been printed in Tagalog. It has probably reached the Phillppines through the medium of Spanish.

Fletcher Gardner.

Bloomington, Ind.

PART V

Some Games of Filipino Children.

Os-Os.

This is a game used by older persons to amuse small children, exactly as our game of the "Five Little Pigs."

The child is grasped by the wrist with the left hand of the elder, who repeats "Ang áma, ang ína, ang káka, ang áli, ang nóno, tóloy, os-os sa kíli-kíli mo." That is, "The father (thumb), the mother (forefinger), the elder brother (middle finger), the elder sister (ring finger), the grandparent (little finger) straight up to your armpit." The armpit is then tickled. Os-os is a verb meaning "to go up stream." This is a common game among the Tagalogs of Mindoro Island.

Marbles.

The game of marbles is played with conical shells, propelled by laying on the ground and striking with the ulnar side of the index finger, which is snapped from the thumb against it. The goal is a hole in the ground, in which the stakes, usually consisting of other shells of the same kind, are deposited. The "taw" is a straight line some six or eight feet away. If a shell is struck, the owner of the striking shell has another shot, and the owner of the shell struck shoots from where he lies. He seems to incur no penalty.

This is a common game on Mindoro, and is played usually at the beginning of the dry season.

Tágo-Tágo.

Translated, the name means, "Play at hiding." It is played exactly as "I spy" and the counting out beforehand is similar. There is a considerable number of counting-out rhymes to be heard, only one of which I am able to give entire. It is in Filipino Spanish. "Pim, pim, serapim, agua, ronda, San Miguel, arcángel."

In English, "Phim, phim, seraphim, water, the night patrol,

St. Michael, the archangel."

Hop-Scotch.

This game is played by marking out in the dust or sand a parallelogram, which is subdivided into a varying number of compartments. A small stone is put into the first subdivision, and the player, standing on one foot, kicks it into each in turn. If it goes out of bounds he is allowed to kick it back, so long as the other foot does not reach the ground. A failure to complete the circuit entails a loss of turn, and on the next round the player begins again at the first compartment.

Jack-stones.

Is played with pebbles or shells. I am unable to give the special movements, which resemble very much our own game. I suspect that it is of Spanish origin.

Fletcher Gardner.

Indianapolis, Ind.

PART VI

Bagobo Myths

By Laura Watson Benedict

The following stories were obtained from the Bagobo people, one of the groups of pagan Malays in southeastern Mindanao, Philippine Islands. Their habitat is on the eastern folds of the Cabadangan mountain-range, in the vicinity of Mount Apo, the highest peak, and on the foothills thence sloping down to the west coast of the Gulf of Davao. They practise a primitive agriculture—raising corn, rice, camotes, and several vegetables—in fields and little gardens at the edge of the forests. Their garments are of home-grown hemp; and their artistic interests centre largely around the decorative designs produced in dyeing, weaving, and embroidery.

In spite of physical barriers interposed by mountain-spurs, frequent swift-flowing rivers, and dense undergrowth in the forests, there is considerable intercourse between the small villages, each of which contains from two to twenty or more houses. The people take long journeys on horse and on foot over the trails to assemble at ceremonial festivals and for purposes of trade, as well as for social visiting. On such occasions, stories and songs are repeated.

That the component parts of the stories have been drawn from numerous and widely separated sources, is apparent, even at a cursory glance. Among these sources, the folk-lore material of Sanscrit writers seems to have left a distinctive impress upon the Bagobo mythical romance. Against a Malay background, and blended with native pagan elements, are presented chains of episodes, characteristic personalities, methods for securing a magical control of the situation, that suggest vividly parallel literary forms in the Sanscrit saga. Still more, one is conscious of a prevailing Indian atmosphere, that may sometimes elude analysis, yet none the less fails not to make itself felt. But as to the line of ethnic contacts which has transfused this peculiar literary quality into Malay myth,—whether it is to be traced solely to the influence exerted by Hindoo religion and Hindoo literature during ages of domination in the Malay archipelago, or whether we must reconsider the hypothesis of an Indonesian migration,—this is a problem of great complexity, for which no satisfactory solution has yet been offered.

Modern foreign increments that have filtered into the stories from the folk-lore of neighboring wild tribes—notably that of the Bilan, the Tagacolo, and, to a less extent, the Culaman and Ata—will have to be sifted out eventually. In illustration of this point, one tale known to be outside of Bagobo sources is here introduced. The story of "Alelu'k and Alebu'tud" was told by an Ata boy to a Bagobo at the coast, who immediately related it to me. It was unquestionably passed on in Bagobo circles, and has become a permanent accession. Yet this was the sole case that came under my observation of a social visit made by an Ata in a Bagobo house; for the Ata live far to the northwest of the Bagobo, and are extremely timid, and "wild" in the popular sense. Recent ethnic influences from higher peoples, pre-eminently the Moro and the Spaniard, will have to be reckoned with. The story of "The Monkey and the Turtle" is clearly modified from a Spanish source.

The myths here presented include only those of which no texts were recorded. A part of the material was given in the vernacular and interpreted by a Bagobo; a part was told in English, or in mixed

English and Bagobo. The stories were taken down in 1907, on Mount Merar in the district of Talun, and at Santa Cruz on the coast.

As regards subject-matter, the stories (ituran) tend to cluster into groups fairly distinguishable in type. Foremost in significance for the cultural tradition of the people is the ulit, a long, romantic tale relating in highly picturesque language the adventures of the mythical Bagobo, who lived somewhere back in the hazy past, before existing conditions were established. Semi-divine some of them were, or men possessing magical power. The old Mona people; the Malaki, who portrayed the Bagobo's ideal of manhood; and the noble lady called Bia,—these and other well-marked characters figure in the ulit.

Another class of stories deals with the demons known as Buso, who haunt graveyards, forests, and rocks. These tales have been built up by numerous accretions from the folk-lore of many generations. The fear of Buso is an ever-present element in the mental associations of the Bagobo, and a definite factor in shaping ritual forms and magical usages. But the story-teller delights to represent Buso as tricked, fooled, brought into embarrassing situations.

Still another type of myth is associated with cosmogony and natural phenomena. It is probable that more extended research would disclose a complete cosmogonic myth to replace the somewhat fragmentary material here offered.

The number of explanatory animal tales thus far collected is surprisingly small. Doubtless there are many more to be gathered. Yet, in view of the comparatively scanty mammalian fauna of Mindanao, we might anticipate a somewhat limited range of animal subjects.

It will be observed that these groups of stories, tentatively thus classified for convenience, are not separated by sharp lines. Buso figures prominently in the ulit; animals play the part of heroes in Buso tales; while in nature myths the traditional Mona are more or less closely associated with the shifting of sky and sun. But this is merely equivalent to saying that all the tales hang together.

A word as to the form of the stories and the manner of narration. Here we find two distinct styles dependent on the content of the myth. The tales of animals, cosmogonic myths, and the folk-lore of Buso, are all told in prose, with many inflections of the voice, and often accompanied by an animated play of dramatic gesture. In marked contrast is the style of the mythical romance, or ulit, which is recited in a rapid monotone, without change of pitch, with no gestures, and with a regard to accent and quantity that gives a rhythmic swing suggestive of a metrical rendering.

Although Bagobo songs are often designated as men's songs and women's songs, in the case of the stories I have found as yet no monopoly by either sex of any special type. The ulit, however, is often told by a young woman just after she leaves the loom, when darkness drops. She sits on the floor, or lies on her back with hands clasped behind her head, and pours out her story in an unbroken flow to the eager young men and girls who gather to listen. Again, I have seen a girl of thirteen the sole auditor while a boy but little older than she rolled off an ulit that seemed interminable, with never a pause for breath. The children did not glance at each other; but the face of each was all alight with joy at the tale.

Myths Associated with Natural Phenomena

Cosmogony

In the beginning, Diwata made the sea and the land, and planted trees of many kinds. Then he took two lumps of earth, and shaped them like human figures; then he spit on them, and they became man and woman. The old man was called Tuglay, and the old woman, Tuglibung. The two were married, and lived together. The Tuglay made a great house, and planted seeds of different kinds that Diwata gave him.

Diwata made the sun, the moon, the stars, and the rivers. First he made the great eel (kasili), a fish that is like a snake in the river, and wound it all around the world. Diwata then made the great crab (kayumang), and put it near the great eel, and let it go wherever it liked. Now, when the great crab bites the great eel, the eel wriggles, and this produces an earthquake.

When the rain falls, it is Diwata throwing out water from the sky. When Diwata spits, the showers fall. The sun makes yellow clouds, and the yellow clouds make the colors of the rainbow. But the white clouds are smoke from the fire of the gods.

In the Days of the Mona

Long ago the sun hung low over the earth. And the old woman called Mona said to the sky, "You go up high, because I cannot pound my rice when you are in the way."

Then the sky moved up higher.

Mona was the first woman, and Tuglay was the first man. There were at that time only one man and one woman on the earth. Their eldest son was named Malaki; their eldest daughter, Bia. They lived at the centre of the earth.

Tuglay and Mona made all the things in the world; but the god made the woman and the man. Mona was also called Tuglibung. Tuglay and Tuglibung got rich, because they could see the god.

But the snake was there too, and he gave the fruit to the man and the woman, saying to them, "If you eat the fruit, it will open your eyes."

Then they both ate the fruit. This made the god angry.

After this, Tuglibung and Tuglay could not see the god any more.

Why the Sky Went Up

In the beginning, when the world was made, the sky lay low down over the earth. At this time the poor families called "Mona" were living in the world. The sky hung so low, that, when they wanted to pound their rice, they had to kneel down on the ground to get a play for the arm. Then the poor woman called Tuglibung said to the sky, "Go up higher! Don't you see that I cannot pound my rice well?"

So the sky began to move upwards. When it had gone up about five fathoms, the woman said again, "Go up still more!"

This made the sun angry at the woman, and he rushed up very high.

In the old days, when the sun as well as the sky was low down, the Mona had a deep hole in the ground, as large as a house, into which they would creep to keep themselves from the fierce heat of the sun.

The Mona were all very old; but after the sun went up very high, they began to get babies.

Why the Sky Went Up

In the beginning, the sky hung so low over the earth, that the people could not stand upright, could not do their work.

For this reason, the man in the sky said to the sky, "Come up!" Then the sky went up to its present place.

The Sun and the Moon

Long ago the Sun had to leave the Moon to go to another town. He knew that his wife, the Moon, was expecting the birth of a child; and, before going away, he said to her, "When your baby is born, if it is a boy, keep it; if a girl, kill it."

A long time passed before the Sun could come back to the Moon, and while he was gone, the Moon gave birth to her baby. It was a girl. A beautiful child it was, with curly hair like binubbud, with burnished nails that looked like gold, and having the white spots called pamoti on its body. The mother felt very sad to think of killing it, and so she hid it in the big box (kaban) where they kept their clothes.

As soon as the Sun returned, he asked the Moon, "How about our baby?"

At once the Moon replied, "It was a girl: I killed it yesterday." The Sun had only a week to stay at home with the Moon. One night he dreamed that a boy with white hair came to him from heaven. The boy stood close to him, and spoke these words:—

"Your wife got a baby, but it was a girl; and she hid it away from you in the box."

When the Sun wakened from sleep, he was very angry at the Moon, and the two fell to quarrelling about the baby. The Moon wanted the child saved.

"You ought to keep it with you," she urged.

"No, no!" protested the Sun. "I cannot keep it, because my body is so hot it would make your baby sick."

"And I cannot keep it," complained the Moon, "for my body is very dark; and that would surely make the child sick."

Then the Sun fell into a passion of rage; and he seized his big kampilan, and slew the child. He cut its small body into numberless little bits,—as many as the grains of sand that lie along the seashore. Out of the window he tossed the pieces of the shining little body; and, as the gleaming fragments sparkled to their places in the sky, the stars came to birth.

Origin of the Stars

All the old Bagobo men say that the Sun and the Moon once had a quarrel about the Moon's baby.

The Moon had a baby in her belly; and the Sun said, "If our baby is a girl, we will kill it, because a girl could not be like me."

Then the Sun went on a journey to another town, and while he was gone, the baby was born; but it was a girl. Now, the Moon felt very sorry to think of her little child being killed, and she hid it in a box. In a few days, the Sun came home to rest with his wife. Then he asked her for the baby.

The Moon answered, "I killed it yesterday: it was a girl."

But the Sun did not believe what his wife said. Then he opened the box to get his clothes, and there he saw a baby-girl. And the Sun was very angry. He seized the baby and cut it into many pieces, and threw the pieces out of the window. Then the pieces of the baby's body became the stars.

Before the Sun and the Moon had their quarrel, they journeyed together through the sky, and the sky was not far above the earth, as now, but it lay low down.

The Fate of the Moon's Baby

The Sun wanted the Moon to have a boy-baby so that it would be like its father. The Moon too hoped to give birth to a boy. But when the child was born, it was a girl. Now, at that time, the Moon was very hungry, and wanted to eat her own baby. Then the Sun killed the girl-child, and ate it up himself.

The Black Men at the Door of the Sun

The men who live in that part of the world near to where the sun rises are very black. They are called Manobo tagselata k'alo. From sunrise until noon, they stay in a hole in the ground to escape the fierce heat of the sun. Just before sunrise, they put their rice in the big pot, with water, and leave it without any fire under the pot. Then they creep into their hole in the ground. The rising sun cooks the rice; and, when the black men come out of the hole at noon, their meal is all ready for them. From noon until sunset, and then all night, the black men play and work. But before the sun rises, they fix their rice in the pot, leave it for the sun to cook, and go down again into the big hole.

Story of the Eclipse

Before time began, very long ago, a great bird called "minokawa" swallowed the moon. Seized with fear, all the people began to scream and make a great noise. Then the bird peeped down to see what was the matter, and he opened his mouth. But as soon as he opened his mouth, the moon sprang out and ran away.

The minokawa-bird is as large as the Island of Negros or Bohol. He has a beak of steel, and his claws too are of steel. His eyes are mirrors, and each single feather is a sharp sword. He lives outside the sky, at the eastern horizon, ready to seize the moon when she reaches there from her journey under the earth.

The moon makes eight holes in the eastern horizon to come out of, and eight holes in the western horizon to go into, because every day the big bird tries to catch her, and she is afraid. The exact moment he tries to swallow her is just when she is about to come in through one of the holes in the east to shine on us again. If the minokawa should swallow the moon, and swallow the sun too, he would then come down to earth and gulp down men also. But when the moon is in the belly of the big bird, and the sky is dark, then all the Bagobo scream and cry, and beat agongs, because they fear they will all "get dead." Soon this racket makes the minokawa-bird look down and "open his mouth to hear the sound." Then the moon jumps out of the bird's mouth and runs away.

All the old men know about the minokawa-bird in the ulit stories.

The "Ulit:" Adventures of Mythical Bagobo at the Dawn of Tradition

Lumabat and Mebu'yan

Long ago Lumabat and his sister (tube') had a quarrel because Lumabat had said, "You shall go with me up into heaven." And his sister had replied, "No, I don't like to do that."

Then they began to fight each other. Soon the woman sat down on the big rice mortar, and said to Lumabat, "Now I am going down below the earth, down to Gimokudan. Down there I shall begin to shake the lemon-tree. Whenever I shake it, somebody up on the earth will die. If the fruit shaken down be ripe, then an old person will die on the earth; but if the fruit fall green, the one to die will be young."

Then she took a bowl filled with pounded rice, and poured the rice into the mortar for a sign that the people should die and go down to Gimokudan. Presently the mortar began to turn round and round while the woman was sitting upon it. All the while, as the mortar was revolving, it was slowly sinking into the earth. But just as it began to settle in the ground, the woman dropped handfuls of the pounded rice upon the earth, with the words: "See! I let fall this rice. This makes many people die, dropping down just like grains of rice. Thus hundreds of people go down; but none go up into heaven."

Straightway the mortar kept on turning round, and kept on going lower down, until it disappeared in the earth, with Lumabat's sister still sitting on it. After this, she came to be known as Mebu'yan. Before she went down below the earth, she was known only as Tube' ka Lumabat ("sister of Lumabat").

Mebu'yan is now chief of a town called Banua Mebu'yan ("Mebu'yan's town"), where she takes care of all dead babies, and gives them milk from her Breasts. Mebu'yan is ugly to look at, for her whole body is covered with nipples. All nursing children who still want the milk, go directly, when they die, to Banua Mebu'yan, instead of to Gimokudan, and remain there with Mebu'yan until they stop taking milk from her breast. Then they go to their own families in Gimokudan, where they can get rice, and "live" very well.

All the spirits stop at Mebu'yan's town, on their way to Gimokudan. There the spirits wash all their joints in the black river that runs through Banua Mebu'yan, and they wash the tops of their heads too. This bathing (pamalugu) is for the purpose of making the spirits feel at home, so that they will not run away and go back to their own bodies. If the spirit could return to its body, the body would get up and be alive again.

Story of Lumabat and Wari

Tuglay and Tuglibung had many children. One of them was called Lumabat. There came a time when Lumabat quarrelled with his sister and was very angry with her. He said, "I will go to the sky, and never come back again."

So Lumabat started for the sky-country, and many of his brothers and sisters went with him. A part of their journey lay over the sea, and when they had passed the sea, a rock spoke to them and said, "Where are you going?"

In the beginning, all the rocks and plants and the animals could talk with the people. Then one boy answered the rock, "We are going to the sky-country."

As soon as he had spoken, the boy turned into a rock. But his brothers and sisters went on, leaving the rock behind.

Presently a tree said, "Where are you going?"

"We are going to the sky," replied one of the girls.

Immediately the girl became a tree. Thus, all the way along the journey, if any one answered, he became a tree, or stone, or rock, according to the nature of the object that put the question.

By and by the remainder of the party reached the border of the sky. They had gone to the very end of the earth, as far as the horizon. But here they had to stop, because the horizon kept moving up and down (supa-supa). The sky and the earth would part, and then close together again, just like the jaws of an animal in eating. This movement of the horizon began as soon as the people reached there.

There were many young men and women, and they all tried to jump through the place where the sky and the earth parted. But the edges of the horizon are very sharp, like a kampilan, and they came together with a snap whenever anybody tried to jump through; and they cut him into two pieces. Then the parts of his body became stones, or grains of sand. One after another of the party tried to jump through, for nobody knew the fate of the one who went before him.

Last of all, Lumabat jumped—quick, quicker than the rest; and before the sharp edges snapped shut, he was safe in heaven. As he walked along, he saw many wonderful things. He saw many kampilans standing alone, and fighting, and that without any man to hold them. Lumabat passed on by them all. Then he came to the town where the bad dead live. The town is called "Kilut." There, in the flames, he saw many spirits with heavy sins on them. The spirits with little sins were not in the flames; but they lay, their bodies covered with sores, in an acid that cuts like the juice of a lemon. Lumabat went on, past them all.

Finally he reached the house of Diwata, and went up into the house. There he saw many diwata, and they were chewing betel-nut, And one diwata spit from his mouth the isse that he had finished chewing. When Lumabat saw the isse coming from the mouth of the god, it looked to him like a sharp knife. Then Diwata laid hold of Lumabat, and Lumabat thought the god held a sharp knife in his hand. But it was no knife: it was just the isse. And Diwata rubbed the isse on Lumabat's belly, and with one downward stroke he opened the belly, and took out Lumabat's intestines (betuka).

Then Lumabat himself became a god. He was not hungry any more, for now his intestines were gone. Yet if he wanted to eat, he had only to say, "Food, come now!" and at once all the fish were there, ready to be caught. In the sky-country, fish do not have to be caught. And Lumabat became the greatest of all the diwata.

Now, when Lumabat left home with his brothers and sisters, one sister and three brothers remained behind. The brother named Wari felt sad because Lumabat had gone away. At last he decided to follow him. He crossed the sea, and reached the border of the sky, which immediately began to make the opening and shutting motions. But Wari was agile, like his brother Lumabat; and he jumped quick, just like Lumabat, and got safe into heaven. Following the same path that his brother had taken, he reached the same house. And again Diwata took the isse, and attempted to open Wari's belly; but Wari protested, for he did not like to have his intestines pulled out. Therefore the god was angry at Wari.

Yet Wari staid on in the house for three days. Then he went out on the atad that joined the front and back part of the gods' house, whence he could look down on the earth. He saw his home town, and it made him happy to look at his fields of sugarcane and bananas, his groves of betel and cocoanuts. There were his bananas ripe, and all his fruits ready to be plucked. Wari gazed, and then he wanted to get back to earth again, and he began to cry; for he did not like to stay in heaven and have his intestines taken out, and he was homesick for his own town.

Now, the god was angry at Wari because he would not let him open his belly. And the god told Wari to go home, and take his dogs with him. First the god fixed some food for Wari to eat on his journey. Then he took meadow-grass (karan), and tied the long blades together, making a line long enough to reach down to earth. He tied Wari and the dogs to one end of the line; but before he lowered the rope, he said to Wari, "Do not eat while you are up in the air, for if you eat, it will set your dogs to quarrelling. If I hear the sound of dogs fighting, I shall let go the rope."

But while Wari hung in the air, he got very hungry, and, although he had been let down only about a third of the distance from heaven to earth, he took some of his food and ate it. Immediately the dogs began to fight. Then Diwata in the sky heard the noise, and he dropped the rope of meadow-grass. Then Wari fell down, down; but he did not strike the ground, for he was caught in the branches of the tree called lanipo. It was a tall tree, and Wari could not get down. He began to utter cries; and all night he kept crying, "Aro-o-o-o-i!" Then he turned into a kulago-bird. At night, when you hear the call of the kulago-bird, you know that it is the voice of Wari.

The kulago-bird has various sorts of feathers, feathers of all kinds of birds and chickens; it has the hair of all animals and the hair of man. This bird lives in very high trees at night, and you cannot see it. You cannot catch it. Yet the old men know a story about a kulago-bird once having been caught while it was building its nest. But this was after there came to be many people on the earth.

The three dogs went right along back to Wari's house. They found Wari's sister and two brothers at home, and staid there with them. After a while, the woman and her two brothers had many children.

"In the beginning," say the old men, "brother and sister would marry each other, just like pigs. This was a very bad custom."

How Man Turned into a Monkey

Before the world was made, the monkey looked like man, and was called manobo, and was actually human. But after the world and people were made, the monkey took its present form.

When people began to live in the world, they had many children. One man was called Lumabat. His father had a number of children, so that Lumabat had many brothers and sisters.

One day a brother of Lumabat was climbing up over the roof, and in his hand he had a long ladle made of cocoanut-shell. He held the ladle behind his back, at the base of his spine, until by and by a tail began to grow. The ladle had turned into a tail, and presently Lumabat's brother became a monkey. After that, a few other people turned into monkeys. But all this came about before Lumabat went to heaven.

The Tuglibung and the Tuglay

Before time began, an old woman (Tuglibung) and an old man (Tuglay) lived in a town at the centre of the world. There came a season of drought, when their bananas spoiled, and all their plants died from the hot sun. Tuglibung and Tuglay were very hungry, and looked skinny, because they had nothing to eat.

One night as the old man slept, he dreamed that a little boy with white hair came close to him, and said, "Much better it would be, if you wouldstay here no longer; much better, that you go to the T'oluk Waig ('water-sources'), where there is a good place to live."

So the old folks started on their journey to the source of the rivers. On their way, they stopped at one place that seemed good, and staid for about a month; but there was little to eat, and they were always hungry. At last, one day, the man climbed up into a tall tree, whence he could see the whole earth, even to the border of the sky. Far away he could see a little smoke, just like a cigarette. Then he climbed "down the tree in a hurry, and told his wife what he had seen.

"I will go and find out where that smoke comes from," he said, "and see if I can get some bananas and things,—all we can eat."

So the man started out and travelled a long way, leaving his wife at home. As he approached the place where he had seen the smoke, he found himself in a vast field full of fruit-trees and sugarcane-plants. The sugarcane grew as big as trees; the bananas were as huge as the trunks of cocoanut-palms; and the papaya-fruit was the size of a great clay jar. He walked on until he reached a very large meadow, full of long wavy grass, where there were many horses and carabao and other animals. Soon after he left the meadow-grass, he could make out, some distance ahead of him, a big house with many smaller houses grouped around it. He was so scared that he could not see the houses very well. He kept his eyes on the ground at his feet.

When he came up to the big house, he saw lying under it piles of human bones. He then knew that the Datu of the Buso lived there. In all the other houses there were buso living too. But he went bravely up the steps of the big house, and sat down on the floor. Right away, while he sat there, the children of Buso wanted to eat him. But Tuglay said, "No, no! don't eat me, because I just came to get bananas of many different kinds."

Then the man made a bargain with the Datu of the Buso, and said, "Give me some bananas, and I will pay you two children for them. Come to my house in nine days, and you shall have one boy and one girl for the bananas." But Tuglay had no children.

Then the Buso gave Tuglay a basket of bananas, and let him go away.

Now, while her husband was away, the woman gave birth to twins,—a boy and a girl. And when the man got home he was pleased, and said, "Oh! that's fine! You got some babies while I was away."

But the man felt very sorry to think of giving his children to the Buso, and he went from place to place, hoping to find some friend who would help him. All the time, the days of the falla ("time of contract") were slipping by. He could get nobody to help him. Now it lacked only two of the nine days' falla. And while the children were asleep, Tuglay said to his wife, "Let us run away, and leave our babies here asleep, because to-morrow the Buso will come."

Then Tuglay and Tuglibung ran away, and left their children. They ran and ran until they reached the T'oluk Waig; but they could not get away from the falla. The nine days of falla had caught up with them.

At home, the children woke up and found no mother and father there, and they began to cry. They thought they would run after their parents. So they left the house, and forded the river, and began to run.

When the nine days were up, the Buso came to Tuglay's house for his pay. When he found nobody at home, he ran after the children, carrying with him many iron axes and big bolos, and accompanied by a crowd of other buso. In all there were three thousand buso,—two thousand walking, and one thousand flying. The children had the start; but the three thousand buso kept gaining on them, until they were close behind.

As they ran, the little boy said to his sister, "When we get to that field over there, where there are ripe bananas, you must not speak a word."

But when they reached the banana-tree, the girl-child cried out,

"Brother, I want to eat a banana."

Then she ate a banana; but she felt so weak she could run no longer. She just lay down and died. Then the boy-child looked about for a place to put his sister's body. He looked at the fine branched trees, full of fruit, and saw that each single fruit was an agong, and the leaves, mother-of-pearl.

To one of the trees, the boy said, "May I put my sister here?" And the tree said that he might do it.

Then the boy laid his sister on a branch of the tree, because the child was dead.

After this, the boy ran back toward the Buso who led the rest, and called out to him, "I'm going to run very fast. Chase me now, and catch me if you can!"

So the boy ran, and the Buso chased him. Hard pressed, the boy sprang toward a big rock, and shouted to it, "O rock, help me! The Buso will catch me."

"Come up!" said the rock, "I'll help you, if I can."

But when the boy climbed up, he found that it was not a rock, but a fine house, that was giving him shelter. In that house lived the Black Lady (Bia t' metum), and she received the boy kindly.

As soon as the Buso came up to the rock, he smiled, and said, "The boy is here all right! I'll break the rock with my axe."

But when he tried to break the rock with axe and poko, the hard stone resisted; and the Buso's tools were blunted and spoiled.

Meantime, in the Black Lady's house the boy was getting ready for a fight, because the Black Lady said, "Go down now; they want you down there."

Then with sharp sword and long spear, bearing a fine war-shield, and wearing ear-plugs of shining ivory, the boy went down to meet the Buso. When he went down the steps, all the other buso had come, and were waiting for him in front of the house. Then they all went to fighting the one boy, and he met them all alone. He fought until every one of the three thousand buso fell down dead. At last, one only of the buso stood up, and he was the great Datu of Buso. But even he fell down before that mighty boy, for none could conquer the boy. He was matulus. After all was done, the boy married the Black Lady, and lived well in her house.

Adventures of the Tuglay

It was eight million (kati) years ago, in the days of the Mona, that the following events took place.

The Tuglay lived in a fine house the walls of which were all mirrored glass, and the roof was hung with brass chains. One day he went out into the woods to snare jungle-fowl, and he slept in the woods all night. The next day, when he turned to go home, he found himself puzzled as to which trail to take. He tried one path after another, but none seemed to lead to his house. At last he said to himself, "I have lost my way: I shall never be able to get home."

Then he walked on at random until he came to a vast field of rice, where great numbers of men were cutting the palay. But the rice-field belonged to Buso, and the harvesters were all buso-men. When they saw Tuglay at the edge of their field, they were glad, and said to one another, "There's a man! We will carry him home."

Then the buso caught Tuglay, and hastened home with him. Now, the great Buso's mansion stretched across the tops of eight million mountains, and very many smaller houses were on the sides of the mountains, all around the great Buso's house; for this was the city of the buso where they had taken Tuglay. As he was carried through the groves of cocoanut-palms on Buso's place, all the Cocoanuts called out, "Tuglay, Tuglay, in a little while the Buso will eat you!"

Into the presence of the great chief of all the buso, they dragged Tuglay. The Datto Buso was fearful to look at. From his head grew one great horn of pure ivory, and flames of fire were blazing from the horn. The Datto Buso questioned the man.

"First of all, I will ask you where you come from, Tuglay."

"I am come from my house in T'oluk Waig," replied the man.

And the great Buso shouted, "I will cut off your head with my sharp kris!"

"But if I choose, I can kill you with your own sword," boldly answered

Tuglay.

Then he lay down, and let the Buso try to cut his neck. The Buso swung his sharp sword; but the steel would not cut Tuglay's neck. The Buso did not know that no knife could wound the neck of Tuglay, unless fire were laid upon his throat at the same time. This was eight million years ago that the Buso tried to cut off the head of Tuglay.

Then another day the Tuglay spoke to all the buso, "It is now my turn: let me try whether I can cut your necks."

After this speech, Tuglay stood up and took from his mouth the chewed betel-nut that is called isse, and made a motion as if he would rub the isse on the great Buso's throat. When the Buso saw the isse, he thought it was a sharp knife, and he was frightened. All the lesser buso began to weep, fearing that their chief would be killed; for the isse appeared to all of them as a keen-bladed knife. The tears of all the buso ran down like blood; they wept streams and streams of tears that all flowed together, forming a deep lake, red in color.

Then Tuglay rubbed the chewed betel on the great Buso's throat. One pass only he made with the isse, and the Buso's head was severed from his body. Both head and body of the mighty Buso rolled down into the great lake of tears, and were devoured by the crocodiles.

Now, the Tuglay was dressed like a poor man,—in bark (bunut) garments. But as soon as he had slain the Buso, he struck a blow at his own legs, and the bark trousers fell off. Then he stamped on the ground, and struck his body, and immediately his jacket and kerchief of bark fell off from him. There he stood, no longer the poor Tuglay, but a Malaki T'oluk Waig, with a gleaming kampilan in his hand.

Then he was ready to fight all the other buso. First he held the kampilan in his left hand, and eight million buso fell down dead. Then he held the kampilan in his right hand, and eight million more buso fell down dead. After that, the Malaki went over to the house of Buso's daughter, who had but one eye, and that in the middle of her forehead. She shrieked with fear when she saw the Malaki coming; and he struck her with his kampilan, so that she too, the woman-buso, fell down dead.

After these exploits, the Malaki T'oluk Waig went on his way. He climbed over the mountains of benati, whose trees men go far to seek, and then he reached the mountains of barayung and balati wood. From these peaks, exultant over his foes, he gave a good war-cry that re-echoed through the mountains, and went up to the ears of the gods. Panguli'li and Salamia'wan heard it from their home in the Shrine of the Sky (Tambara ka Langit), and they said, "Who chants the song of war (ig-sungal)? Without doubt, it is the Malak T'oluk Waig, for none of all the other malaki could shout just like that."

His duty performed, the Malaki left the ranges of balati and barayung, walked down toward the sea, and wandered along the coast until he neared a great gathering of people who had met for barter. It was market-day, and all sorts of things were brought for trade. Then the Malaki T'oluk Waig struck his legs and his chest, before the people caught sight of him; and immediately he was clothed in his old bark trousers and jacket and kerchief, just like a poor man. Then he approached the crowd, and saw the people sitting on the ground in little groups, talking, and offering their things for sale.

The Malaki Lindig Ramut ka Langit and all the other malaki from the surrounding country were there. They called out to him, "Where are you going?"

The Tuglay told them that he had got lost, and had been travelling a long distance. As he spoke, he noticed, sitting among a group of young men, the beautiful woman called Moglung.

She motioned to him, and said, "Come, sit down beside me."

And the Tuglay sat down on the ground, near the Moglung. Then the woman gave presents of textiles to the Malaki Lindig Ramut ka Langit and the other malaki in her crowd. But to the Tuglay she gave betel-nut that she had prepared for him.

After that, the Moglung said to all the malaki, "This time I am going to leave you, because I want to go home."

And off went the Moglung with the Tuglay, riding on the wind. After many days, the Moglung and the Tuglay rested on the mountains of barayung, and, later, on the mountains of balakuna-trees. From these heights, they looked out over a vast stretch of open country, where the deep, wavy meadow-grass glistened like gold; and pastured there were herds of cows and carabao and many horses. And beyond rose another range of mountains, on the highest of which stood the Moglung's house. To reach it they had to cross whole forests of cocoanut and betel-nut trees that covered eight million mountains. Around the house were all kinds of useful plants and trees. When they walked under the floor of the house, the Moglung said, "My grandmother is looking at me because I have found another grandchild for her."

Then the grandmother (Tuglibung) called to them, saying, "Come up, come up, my grandchildren!"

As soon as they entered the house, the Tuglay sat down in a corner of the kitchen, until the grandmother offered him a better place, saying, "Do not stay in the kitchen. Come and sleep on my bed."

The Tuglay rested eight nights in the grandmother's bed. At the end of the eight nights the Moglung said to him, "Please take this betel-nut that I have prepared for you."

At first Tuglay did not want to take it; but the next day, when the Moglung again offered the betel, he accepted it from her and began to chew. After that, the Tuglay took off his trousers of bark and his jacket of bark, and became a Malaki T'oluk Waig. But the Moglung wondered where the Tuglay had gone, and she cried to her grandmother, "Where is the Tuglay?"

But the Malaki stood there, and answered her, "I am the Tuglay." At first the Moglung was grieved, because the Malaki seemed such a grand man, and she wanted Tuglay back.

But before long the Malaki said to her, "I want you to marry me." So they were married. Then the Moglung opened her gold box, and took out a fine pair of trousers (saroa'r) and a man's jacket (umpak ka mama), and gave them to the Malaki as a wedding-gift.

When they had been living together for a while, there came a day when the Malaki wanted to go and visit a man who was a great worker in brass,—the Malaki Tuangun; and the Moglung gave him directions for the journey, saying, "You will come to a place where a hundred roads meet. Take the road that is marked with the prints of many horses and carabao. Do not stop at the place of the crossroads, for if you stop, the Bia who makes men giddy will hurt you."

Then the Malaki went away, and reached the place where a hundred roads crossed, as Moglung had said. But he stopped there to rest and chew betel-nut. Soon he began to feel queer and dizzy, and he fell asleep, not knowing anything. When he woke up, he wandered along up the mountain until he reached a house at the border of a big meadow, and thought he would stop and ask his way. From under the house he called up, "Which is the road to the Malaki Tuangun?"

It was the Bia's voice that answered, "First come up here, and then

I'll tell you the road."

So the Malaki jumped up on the steps and went in. But when he was inside of her house, the Bia confessed that she did not know the way to the Malaki Tuangun's house.

"I am the woman," she said, "who made you dizzy, because I wanted to have you for my own."

"Oh! that's the game," said the Malaki. "But the Moglung is my wife, and she is the best woman in the world."

"Never mind that," smiled the Bia. "Just let me comb your hair." Then the Bia gave him some betel-nut, and combed his hair until he grew sleepy. But as he was dropping off, he remembered a certain promise he had made his wife, and he said to the Bia, "If the Moglung comes and finds me here, you be sure to waken me."

After eight days had passed from the time her husband left home, the Moglung started out to find him, for he had said, "Eight days from now I will return."

By and by the Moglung came to the Bia's house, and found the Malaki there fast asleep; but the Bia did not waken him. Then the Moglung took from the Malaki's toes his toe-rings (paniod), and went away, leaving a message with the Bia:—

"Tell the Malaki that I am going back home to find some other malaki: tell him that I'll have no more to do with him."

But the Moglung did not go to her own home: she at once started for her brother's house that was up in the sky-country.

Presently the Malaki woke up, and when he looked at his toes, he found that his brass toe-rings were gone.

"The Moglung has been here!" he cried in a frenzy. "Why didn't you waken me, as I told you?" Then he seized his sharp-bladed kampilan, and slew the Bia. Maddened by grief and rage, he dashed to the door and made one leap to the ground, screaming, "All the people in the world shall fall by my sword!"

On his war-shield he rode, and flew with the wind until he came to the horizon. Here lived the Malaki Lindig Ramut ka Langit. And when the two malaki met, they began to fight; and the seven brothers of the Malaki Lindig that live at the edge of the sky, likewise came out to fight. But when the battle had gone on but a little time, all the eight malaki of the horizon fell down dead. Then the angry Malaki who had slain the Bia and the eight young men went looking for more people to kill; and when he had shed the blood of many, he became a buso with only one eye in his forehead, for the buso with one eye are the worst buso of all. Everybody that he met he slew.

After some time, he reached the house of the great priest called "Pandita," and the Pandita checked him, saying, "Stop a minute, and let me ask you first what has happened to make you like this."

Then the Buso-man replied sadly, "I used to have a wife named Moglung, who was the best of all the bia; but when I went looking for the Malaki Tuangun, that other Bia made me dizzy, and gave me betel, and combed my hair. Then she was my wife for a little while. But I have killed her, and become a buso, and I want to kill all the people in the world."

"You had better lie down on my mat here, and go to sleep," advised the Pandita. While the Buso slept, the Pandita rubbed his joints with betel-nut; and when he woke up, he was a malaki again.

Then the Pandita talked to him, and said, "Only a few days ago, the Moglung passed here on her way to her brother's home in heaven. She went by a bad road, for she would have to mount the steep rock-terraces. If you follow, you will come first to the Terraces of the Wind (Tarasu'ban ka Kara'mag), then you reach the Terraces of Eight-fold Darkness (Walu Lapit Dukilum), and then the Terraces of the Rain (Tarasuban k'Udan).

Eagerly the Malaki set out on his journey, with his kabir on his back, and his betel-nut and buyo-leaf in the kabir. He had not travelled far, before he came to a steep ascent of rock-terraces,—the Terraces of the Wind, that had eight million steps. The Malaki knew not how to climb up the rocky structure that rose sheer before him, and so he sat down at the foot of the ascent, and took his kabir off his back to get out some betel-nut. After he had begun to chew his betel, he began to think, and he pondered for eight days how he could accomplish his hard journey. On the ninth day he began to jump up the steps of the terraces, one by one. On each step he chewed betel, and then jumped again; and at the close of the ninth day he had reached the top of the eight million steps, and was off, riding on his shield.

Next he reached the sharp-edged rocks called the "Terraces of Needles" (Tarasuban ka Simat), that had also eight million steps. Again he considered for eight days how he could mount them. Then on the ninth day he sprang from terrace to terrace, as before, chewing betel-nut on each terrace, and left the Tarasuban ka Simat, riding on his shield. Then he arrived at the Terraces of Sheet-Lightning (Tarasuban ka Dilam-dilam); and he took his kabir off his back, and prepared a betel-nut, chewed it, and meditated for eight days. On the ninth day he jumped from step to step of the eight million terraces, and went riding off on his war-shield. When he reached the Terraces of Forked-Lightning (Tarasuban ka Kirum), he surmounted them on the ninth day, like the others.

But now he came to a series of cuestas named "Dulama Bolo Kampilan," because one side of each was an abrupt cliff with the sharp edge of a kampilan; and the other side sloped gradually downward, like a blunt-working bolo. How to cross these rocks, of which there were eight million, the Malaki did not know; so he stopped and took off his kabir, cut up his betel-nut, and thought for eight days. Then on the ninth day he began to leap over the rocks, and he kept on leaping for eight days, each day jumping over one million of the cuestas. On the sixteenth day he was off, riding on his shield. Then he reached the Terraces of the Thunder (Tarasuban ka Kilat), which he mounted, springing from one terrace to the next, as before, after he had meditated for eight days. Leaving these behind him on the ninth day, he travelled on to the Mountains of Bamboo (Pabungan Kawayanan), covered with bamboo whose leaves were all sharp steel. These mountains he could cross without the eight days' thought, because their sides sloped gently. From the uplands he could see a broad sweep of meadow beyond, where the grass glistened like gold. And when he had descended, and walked across the meadow, he had to pass through eight million groves of cocoanut-trees, where the fruit grew at the height of a man's waist, and every cocoanut had the shape of a bell (korung-korung). Then he reached a forest of betel-nut, where again the nuts could be plucked without the trouble of climbing, for the clusters grew at the height of a man's waist. Beyond, came the meadows with white grass, and plants whose leaves were all of the rare old embroidered cloth called tambayang. He then found himself at the foot-hills of a range of eight million mountains, rising from the heart of the meadows, and, when he had climbed to their summit, he stood before a fine big house.

From the ground he called out, "If anybody lives in this house, let him come look at me, for I want to find the way to the Shrine in the Sky, or to the Little Heaven, where my Moglung lives."

But nobody answered.

Then the Malaki sprang up the bamboo ladder and looked in at the door, but he saw no one in the house. He was weary, after his journey, and sat down to rest in a chair made of gold that stood there. Soon there came to his ears the sound of men's voices, calling out, "There is the Malaki T'oluk Waig in the house."

The Malaki looked around the room, but there was no man there, only a little baby swinging in its cradle. Outside the house were many malaki from the great town of Lunsud, and they came rushing in the door, each holding a keen blade without handle (sobung). They all surrounded the Malaki in the gold chair, ready to fight him. But the Malaki gave them all some betel-nut from his kabir, and made the men friendly toward him. Then all pressed around the Malaki to look at his kabir, which shone like gold. They had never before seen a man's bag like this one. "It is the kabir of the Malaki T'oluk Waig," they said. The Malaki slept that night with the other malaki in the house.

When morning came, the day was dark, like night, for the sun did not shine. Then the Malaki took his kampilan and stuck it into his belt, and sat down on his shield. There was no light on the next day, nor on the next. For eight days the pitchy darkness lasted; but on the ninth day it lifted. Quick from its cradle jumped the baby, now grown as tall as the bariri-plant; that is, almost knee-high.

"Cowards, all of you!" cried the child to the Malaki Lunsud. "You are no malaki at all, since you cannot fight the Malaki T'oluk Waig." Then, turning to the Malaki T'oluk Waig, the little fellow said, "Please teach me how to hold the spear."

When the Malaki had taught the boy how to make the strokes, the two began to fight; for the boy, who was called the Pangalinan, was eager to use his spear against the Malaki. But the Malaki had magical power (matulus), so that when the Pangalinan attacked him with sword or spear, the blades of his weapons dissolved into water. For eight million days the futile battle went on. At last the Pangalinan gave it up, complaining to the Malaki T'oluk Waig, "How can I keep on fighting you, when every time I hit you my knives turn to water?"

Disheartened, the Pangalinan threw away his spear and his sword. But the Malaki would not hurt the Pangalinan when they were fighting; and as soon as the boy had flung his weapons outside the house, the Malaki put his arm around him and drew him close. After that, the two were friends.

One day the Pangalinan thought he would look inside the big gold box that stood in the house. It was his mother's box. The boy went and raised the lid, but as soon as the cover was lifted, his mother came out from the box. After this had happened, the Pangalinan got ready to go and find the Moglung whom the Malaki had been seeking. The boy knew where she lived, for he was the Moglung's little brother (tube'). He took the bamboo ladder that formed the steps to the house, and placed it so that it would reach the Shrine in the Sky, whither the Moglung had gone. Up the bamboo rounds he climbed, until he reached the sky and found his sister. He ran to her crying, "Quick! come with me! The great Malaki T'oluk Waig is down there."

Then the Moglung came down from heaven with her little brother to their house where the Malaki was waiting for her. The Moglung and the Malaki were very happy to meet again, and they slept together that night.

Next day the Moglung had a talk with the Malaki, and said, "Now I want to live with you; but you remember that other woman, Maguay Bulol, that you used to sleep with. You will want her too, and you had better send for her."

So the Malaki summoned Maguay Bulol, and in a few minutes Maguay Bulol was there. Then the Malaki had two wives, and they all lived in the same house forever.

The Tuglay and the Bia

Long ago, in the days of the Mona, the Tuglay lived on a high mountain. He lived very well, for his cocoanut-trees grew on both sides of the mountain. But he had no hemp-plants, and so he had to make his clothes of the soft dry sheath that covers the trunk of the cocoanut-palm (bunut). This stuff caught fire easily, and many a time his clothes ignited from the flame where his dinner was cooking, and then he would have to make fresh garments from bunut.

One day he looked from his house over the neighboring mountains, and saw the village of Koblun. He thought it looked pretty in the distance. Then he looked in another direction, and saw the town of the Malaki Tuangun, and said, "Ah! that is just as nice looking as the Koblun town. I will go and see the town of the Malaki Tuangun."

Immediately he got ready for the journey. He took his spear (that was only half a spear, because the fire had burned off a part of the handle) and his shield, that was likewise only half a shield. He started out, and walked on and on until he reached the mountains called "Pabungan Mangumbiten."

Now, on another mountain there lived a young man named the Malaki Itanawa, with his little sister. They lived alone together, for they were orphans. The young girl said to her brother, "Let us travel over the mountains to-day."

And the boy answered, "Yes, my sister, we will go."

And the two climbed over the hills, and they reached the Pabungan Mangumbiten soon after the Tuglay. And they were astonished to see the great Tuglay. But when the Tuglay saw the young girl, who was named Bia Itanawa Inelu, he was so bewildered and startled that he turned away his eyes, and could not look at the sister and brother.

Then the girl prepared a betel-nut and offered it to the Tuglay, but he did not like to accept it. But when she had pressed it upon him many times, he took the betel and chewed it.

Then the girl said, "Come with my brother and me to my house, for we have no companion."

But when the girl saw the Tuglay hesitate, she asked him, "Where were you going when we met you?"

The Tuglay answered, "I want to go to the town of the Malaki Tuangun, for to my home has come the word that the Malaki is a mighty man, and his sister a great lady."

Then the girl looked at the Tuglay, and said, "If you want to make ready to go to the Malaki Tuangun's town, you ought to put on your good trousers and a nice jacket."

At that, the Tuglay looked mournful; for he was a poor man, and had no fine clothes. Then, when the girl saw how the case stood, she called for beautiful things, such as a malaki wears,—fine hemp trousers, beaded jacket, good war-shield and brass-bound spear, ear-plugs of pure ivory, and eight necklaces of beads and gold. Straightway at the summons of the Bia, all the fine things appeared; and the Tuglay got ready to go away. He was no longer the poor Tuglay. His name was now the Malaki Dugdag Lobis Maginsulu. Like two big moons, his ivory ear-plugs shone; when he moved his shield, flames of living fire shot from it; and when he held up his spear, the day would grow dark, because he was a brave man. His new clothes he sent upon the swift wind to the Malaki Tuangun's town.

When the Tuglay started, the Bia gave him her own brass betel-box (katakia) to take with him. It was a katakia that made sounds, and was called a "screaming katakia."

"May I eat the betel-nut from your box?" asked the man; and she replied, "Yes, but do not throw away the other things in the box."

The Malaki Dugdag Lobis Maginsulu walked on until he reached the town of the Malaki Tuangun, and sat down on the ground before the house. The Malaki Tuangun was a great brass-smith: he made katakia and other objects of brass, and hence was called the Malaki Tuangun Katakia. As soon as he heard the other malaki call from outside, "May I come up into your house?" he sent down eight of his slaves to look and see who wanted to visit him.

And the eight slaves brought word to their master that the Malaki

Dugdag Lobis Maginsulu waited to enter.

Then the Malaki Tuangun Katakia called to his visitor, "Come up, if you can keep from bringing on a fight, because there are many showers in my town."

Then the other malaki went up the steps into the house, and the Malaki Tuangun said to him, "You shall have a good place to sit in my house,—a place where nobody ever sat before."

Then the Malaki Tuangun prepared a betel-nut for his guest. But the Malaki Dugdag Lobis Maginsulu would not take the betel-nut from him. So the Malaki Tuangun called his sister, who was called Bia Tuangun Katakia, and said to her, "You go outside and prepare a betel-nut for the Malaki."

As soon as the Bia had finished preparing the betel, she took the (screaming?) katakia from the Malaki, and set it on the floor. Then the Malaki Dugdag Lobis Maginsulu took the betel-nut from the lady. When he had finished chewing it, he stood up and went to the place where the Bia Tuangun Katakia was sitting, and he lay down beside her, and said, "Come, put away your work, and comb my hair."

"No, I don't like to comb your hair," she replied.

The Malaki was displeased at this retort, so at last the woman agreed to comb his hair, for she did not want to see the Malaki angry. By and by the Malaki felt sleepy while his hair was being combed; and he said to the Bia, "Do not wake me up."

He fell asleep, and did not waken until the next day. Then he married the Bia Tuangun Katakia.

After they had been married for three months, the Bia said to the Malaki, "The best man I know is the Manigthum. He was my first husband."

But the Manigthum had left home, and had gone off to do some big fighting. He killed the Malaki Taglapida Pabungan, and he killed the Malaki Lindig Ramut ka Langit.

After the Manigthum had slain these great men, he came back to the home of his wife. When he came near the house he saw, lying down on the ground under the kinarum-tree, the things that he had given his wife before he went away,—pendants of pearl, bracelets and leglets of brass, gold necklaces (kamagi), hair-ornaments of dyed goats'-hair and birds'-down, finger-rings, and leg-bands of twisted wire hung with bells. As he looked at the beautiful ornaments all thrown on the ground, he heard the voice of the Malaki Dugdag Lobis Manginsulu calling to him, "Do not come up, because your wife is mine."

Then the two malaki went to fighting with sword and spear. After a sharp fight, the Manigthum was killed, and the Malaki Dugdag Lobis Maginsulu had the Bia for his wife.

The Malaki's Sister and the Basolo

There is a certain mountain that has a sharp, long crest like a kampilan. Up on this mountain stretched many fields of hemp, and groves of cocoanut-palms, that belonged to the Malaki and his sister.

Near to these hemp-fields lived the Basolo-man, under a tall barayung-tree. His little house was full of venison and pig-meat and lard, and he kept a dog to hunt pigs and deer. Although his hut looked small and poor, the Basolo possessed treasures of brass and beads and fine textiles. He had a kabir, from which darted forked lightning; and in the bag was a betel-box and a necklace of pure gold.

One day when the Malaki's sister went to look at her hemp, she felt curious to go inside the Basolo's house. The Basolo was lying on the floor, fast asleep, when the woman entered. She looked at the things in the house, and saw hanging on the wall the Basolo's bag with the lightning playing on it. Now the bag was an old one, and had a lot of mud in it; but the woman thought it must be full of gold, because the lightning never ceased to flash from it. So she crept across the floor, and took the bag from off the end of the bamboo slat on which it hung. Still the Basolo slept, and still the lightning continued to play upon the bag. The woman looked inside the bag and saw a fine gold betel-box, and when she lifted the lid, there in the box lay a necklace of pure gold. Swiftly she closed the box, and stealthily drew it out of the bag. Into the folds of her hemp skirt she slipped the precious box with the gold necklace inside, and very quietly ran down the bamboo ladder at the house-door.

When she got home, her brother smiled, and said to her, "What has happened to you, my sister?"

Bright flashes of lightning seemed to be coming from the girl. She looked almost as if she were made of gold, and the lightning could not escape from her. Then she took out the betel-box and the necklace, and showed them to her brother, saying that she had found them in the Basolo's hut.

The Basolo awoke, and found his brass katakia and his fine necklace gone.

"Who has been here?" he cried.

In a frenzy he hunted through his kabir, throwing out of it his old work-knife and his rusty spear-head and all the poor things that he kept in his bag. Then he began to moan and weep for his betel-box and gold necklace.

By and by he started out to find his lost things. In the soft soil close to the house, he found the footprints of the woman; and, following the prints, he traced her to the Malaki's house. Right there the footprints ended. The Basolo stood at the foot of the steps, and called, "Who has been in my house?"

Then he ran up the ladder and rushed into the house, screaming to the Malaki's sister, "Give me back my gold necklace! If you don't give it back, I'll marry you."

Quick came the woman's answer, "I don't like you, and I will not marry you."

But her brother was angry because she refused to marry the Basolo. At last she agreed to the match, and said to the Basolo, "Yes, I will marry you; but I can't let you live in my house. You must stay in your own house over yonder."

So the Basolo and the Malaki's sister agreed to meet and try each other (talabana). Then the Basolo went home.

Not long after this, there came a day when many men went out to hunt the wild pig and the deer. And from her house the woman heard the sound of many men gathering in the meadow. There were Malaki T'oluk Waig and other malaki, who were there ready for the chase. And the girl thought, "I will go out and see the men."

Immediately she hurried to dress herself carefully. She put on nine waists one over another, and similarly nine skirts (panapisan); and then she girded herself with a chain of brass links that went a thousand times round her waist. Over her left shoulder she hung her small beaded basket (kambol) that was decorated with row upon row of little tinkling bells, a million in all, and each bell as round as a pea.

But the Basolo knew that the girl was dressing to go out, and he was angry that she should want to go where there were so many men gathered. In order to keep watch on her movements, he climbed up into a hiding-place behind the great leaves of an areca-palm, and waited. Presently he saw the woman walking to the meadow. And she staid there just one night. But the Malaki was alarmed when he found that his sister had gone out to see the men. And after he had taken off his clothes, he began to put them on again to follow his sister.

Then, when the girl's brother and all the other malaki had assembled in the meadow, the Basolo came down from the tree and went home. When he got into his house, he took off his coat, and became a Malaki T'oluk Waig. His body shone like the sun (you could hardly look at him), and all his garments were of gold. He had on nine jackets, one over another, and nine pairs of trousers. Then he called for his horse, whose name was Kambeng Diluk; and Kambeng neighed into the air, and waited, prancing, before the house. Soon the Malaki T'oluk Waig mounted his horse, and sitting on a saddle of mirrored glass, he rode toward the meadow. Then Kambeng Diluk began to run, just like the wind.

When they reached the meadow, there were many people there. The Malaki's wife was sitting on the grass, with men grouped around her, and she was laughing with them. But she did not recognize her husband when he came riding up. After everybody had arrived, they set fire to the long grass, and burned off the meadow, so as to bring the wild pigs and the deer out of ambush. Then many men entered the chase and ran their horses; but none could catch the deer or the wild boar, except only the great Malaki, who had been the Basolo: he alone speared much game.

When the burning of the meadow and the hunt were finished, many men wanted to marry the Malaki T'oluk Waig's wife, and many of them embraced her. But the Malaki T'oluk Waig stood up, fierce with passion. His body was almost like a flame to look at. And he fought the other malaki, and killed many, until at last all were dead but one, and that was the woman's brother.

When all was done, the Malaki mounted his horse and rode back to his home. His house was all of gold, and yet it looked just like a mean little hut nestled under the barayung-tree. Then the Malaki picked up his coat and put it on: at once he became a Basolo again. He then went over to the woman's house and waited there for her to come back. By and by she came loitering along, crying all the way, because she was afraid to meet her husband. But the Basolo staid right along in the house, and lived with the woman and her brother. Then, after they had tried each other, they were married with Bagobo ceremony. The Basolo took off his coat, and again became a Malaki T'oluk Waig. They lived well in their house, and they had a big hacienda of hemp and cocoanuts and banana-plants.

The Mona

When the Mona lived on the earth, there was a certain man who said to his wife, "I want to go out and make some traps."

So that day he went out and made about thirty traps, of sticks with nooses attached, to snare jungle-fowl. His work finished, he returned home. Next day he went out to look at his traps, but found that he had caught, not a wild chicken, but a big lizard (palas) with pretty figured patterns on its back. The man said to the lizard, "Halloo!"

Then he released the lizard, and gave him his own carrying-bag and work-knife, and told him to go straight to his house. But the lizard was afraid to go to the man's house, for he suspected that the man wanted to make a meal of him. Instead, he ran up a tree, taking with him the knife and the bag. The tree overhung a clear brook, and the lizard could see his reflection (alung) in the water.

No fowl could the man snare that day, and he went home. As soon as he reached the house, he said to his wife, "Are you all done cleaning that lizard?"

"What lizard are you talking about?" returned the woman. "There's no lizard here."

"I sent one here," insisted the man, "and I'm hungry."

"We have no lizard," repeated his wife.

In a hot temper the man went back to his traps, and there saw the tracks of the lizard, leading, not towards his house, but exactly in the opposite direction. Following the tracks, he reached the brook, and at once caught sight of the lizard's reflection in the water. Immediately the man jumped into the water, grasping for the image of the slippery lizard; but he had to jump out again with empty hands. He tried again. Hour after hour he kept on jumping, until he got so wet and cold that he had to give it up and go home.

"The lizard is right over there in the brook," he told his wife; "but I could not get hold of him."

"I'll go and look at him with you," she said.

So together they reached the brook; and the woman glanced first into the water, and then up into the tree.

"You foolish man," she smiled. "Look in the tree for your lizard. That's just his shadow (alung) in the water."

The man looked up, and saw the lizard in the tree. Then he started to climb up the trunk, but found himself so chilled and stiff from jumping into the water, that he kept slipping down whenever he tried

to climb. Then the woman took her turn, and got part way up the tree. The man looked up at his wife, and noticed that she had sores on parts of her body where she could not see them, and he called to her, "Come down! don't climb any higher; you've got sores." So she climbed down.

Then her husband wanted to get some medicine out of his bag to give her for the sores; but the lizard had his bag.

"Throw down my bag and knife to me!" he shouted up to the lizard, "because I must get busy about fixing medicine for my wife." And the lizard threw down to him his knife and his bag.

As soon as they got home, the man made some medicine for his wife; but the sores did not heal. Then he went to his friend Tuglay and said, "What is the medicine for my wife?"

Tuglay went home with the man; and when they reached the house, he told him what he was about to do. "Look!" said the Tuglay.

Then the man looked, and saw the Tuglay go to his wife and consort with her.

And the husband let him do it, for he said to himself, "That is the medicine for my wife."

When the Tuglay was done with the woman, he said, "Go now to your wife."

Then the man went to her, and said, "This is the best of all." After that, the man cared for nothing except to be with his wife. He did not even care to eat. He threw out of the house all the food they had,—the rice, the sugarcane, the bananas, and all of their other things. He threw them far away. But after they had taken no food for several days, the man and the woman began to grow thin and weak. Still they did not try to get food, because they wanted only to gratify their passion for each other. At last both of them got very skinny, and finally they died.

Folk-Lore of the Buso

How to See the Buso

The Buso live in the great branching trees and in the graveyard. The night after a person has been buried, the Buso dig up the body with their claws, and drink all the blood, and eat the flesh. The bones they leave, after eating all the flesh off from them. If you should go to the graveyard at night, you would hear a great noise. It is the sound of all the Buso talking together as they sit around on the ground, with their children playing around them. You cannot see the Buso; but if you do get a glimpse of one of them, it is only for a few minutes. He looks like a shadow.

In the beginning, everybody could see the Buso, because then the Buso and the people were friendly together. Nobody died in those days, for the Buso helped the men, and kept them from dying. But many years ago the Buso and man had a quarrel, and after that nobody could see the Buso any more.

Now, there is one way to see Buso; but a man must be very brave to do it. While the coffin for a dead man is being made, if you cut some chips from it and carry them to the place where the tree was felled for the box, and lay the chips on the stump from which the wood was cut, and then go again on the night of the funeral to the same place, you will see Buso. Stand near the stump, and you will see passing before you (1) a swarm of fireflies; (2) the intestines of the dead person; (3) many heads of the dead person; (4) many arms of the dead person; (5) many legs of the dead person; (6) the entire body passing before you; (7) shadows flitting before you; and finally (8) the Buso. But no one yet has been brave enough to try it.

"But one thing I did when my uncle died," said my boy informant. "I chipped a piece of wood from the coffin, and tied it to a long string, like a fly to a fish-hook. This I let down between the slats of the floor, as I stood in the room where the dead body lay, and I held the line dangling. As a fish catches at the bait, so Buso seized that bit of wood, and for about two minutes I could feel him pulling at it from under the house. Then I drew up the string with the wood. Buso was there under the house, and smelt the chip from the coffin."

Buso and the Woman

In a little house there lived a man and his wife together. One night, after they had been married for a long time, the man told his wife that he would like to go fishing.

"Oh, yes! my husband," said the woman eagerly. "Go, and bring me some nice fish to-morrow, so that we can have a good meal."

The man went out that same night to fish. And his wife was left alone in the house.

In the night, while her husband was away, the Buso came, and tried to pass himself off as her husband, saying, "You see I am back. I got no fish, because I was afraid in the river." Then the Buso-man made a great fire, and sat down by it.

But the woman did not believe that it was her husband. So she hid

her comb in a place on the floor, and she said to her comb, "If the

Buso calls me, do you answer. Tell him that I have run away because

I have great fear of the Buso."

Then, when the Buso called, the Comb answered just as the woman had told it. By and by the Buso went away. In the morning, the man came back from fishing, because daylight had come. And he had a fine catch of fish. Then the woman told him all that had happened, and the man never again let his wife sleep alone in the house. After that, everything went well; for Buso was afraid of the man, and never again attempted to come there.

The Buso's Basket

Two children went out into the field to tend their rice-plants. They said these words to keep the little birds away from the grain:—

"One, one, maya-bird,

Yonder in the north;

Keep off from eating it,

This my rice."

Just then they heard the sound of a voice, calling from the great pananag-tree, "Wait a minute, children, until I make a basket for you."

"What is that?" said the boy to his sister.

"Oh, nothing!" answered the little girl. "It's the sound of something."

Then the children called to their father and mother; but only from the pananag-tree the answer came, "Just wait till I finish this basket to hold you in."

Down, then, from the tree came the great Buso, with a big, deep basket (such as women carry bananas and camotes in) hanging from his shoulders. The frightened children did not dare to run away; and Buso sat down near by in the little hut where the rice was kept. Soon he said to the children, "Please comb out my nice hair."

But, when they tried to comb his hair, they found it swarming with big lice and worms.

"Well, let's go on now," said the Buso. Then he stuffed the children into his deep burden-basket, and swung the basket upon his back.

On the instant the little girl screamed out, "Wait a minute, Buso! I've dropped my comb. Let me down to pick it up."

So the Buso sat down on the ground, and let the girl climb out of the basket. He sat waiting for her to find her comb; but all the time she was picking up big stones, and putting them into the basket. Her brother got out of the basket too, and then both girl and boy climbed up into a tall betel-nut tree, leaving Buso with a basket full of stones on his back.

Up to his house in the pananag-tree went Buso with the heavy basket. When his wife saw him, she laughed and shouted very loud. She was glad, because she thought there was a man in the basket, all ready to eat. But, when Buso slipped the basket down from his shoulders, there was no human flesh in it, but only big stones.

Then the angry Buso hurried back to look for the two children. At last he caught sight of them far up in the betel-nut tree, and wondered how he could get them. Now, at the foot of the tree there was a growth of the wild plant called "bagkang;" and Buso said words to make the bagkang grow faster and taller:—

"Tubu, tubu, bagkang,

Grow, grow, bagkang,

Baba, baba mamaa'n."

Handle, handle, betel-nut.

But the children, in their turn, said:—

"Tubu, tubu, mamaa'n,

Grow, grow, betel-nut,

Baba, baba bagkang."

Handle, handle, bagkang.

By and by, when the bagkang-stems had grown so tall as almost to reach the clusters of betel-nuts at the top of the trunk, the boy and girl said to each other. "Let us pick betel-nuts, and throw them down on the bagkang."

And as soon as they began to pick, the betel-nuts became so big and heavy that the bagkang-plants fell down when the betel-nuts dropped on them.

Then the Buso went away; and the children climbed down in haste, ran home, and told their mother and father how the Buso had tried to carry them off.

The Buso-Child

Datu Ayo was a great man among the Bagobo, well known throughout the mountain-country for his bravery and his riches. He had gathered in his house many products of Bagobo workmanship in textiles and brass and fine weapons. At his death, human sacrifices of slaves were offered up for him. It was not many years ago that he went down to the great city of the dead, and many of his children and grandchildren are living now. His sons like to think about their father's renown; and, as a reminder, the eldest son, Kawayun, always kept in his medicine-case two of the incisor teeth of the great Ayo, until he needed money, and sold the medicine-case with its contents. It had made Kawayun happy to look at his father's teeth.

When Datu Ayo died, his wife was about to become a mother. Now, the Bagobo women know that, when they become pregnant, they must be very careful to protect themselves from the evil Buso. On going to bed at night, an expectant mother places near her the woman's knife (gulat), the kampilan, and all the other knives, to frighten Buso away. Failing this, the Buso will come to the woman while she sleeps, and change her baby into a Buso-child. One night, the wife of Datu Ayo lay down to sleep without putting any knives near her; and that very night the Buso came, and he transformed her child into a Buso-child. She did not know when he came, nor did she even think that a Buso had been near her, until her baby was born.

Everybody around the woman at the birth saw that something was the matter with the child. It was little and frail, and as weak as threads of cotton. Its body was flat, and its legs and arms were helpless and flabby. Then all the men said, "That is a Buso-child."

As the little boy grew old enough to creep, he moved just like a fish, with a sort of wriggling motion. He could not stand on his feet, for his legs were too weak to support his body; and he could not sit down, but only lie flat. He could never be dressed in umpak and saroa'r, and his body remained small and puny.

Now the boy is more than fourteen years old, but he cannot walk a step. He understands very well what is said to him, and he can talk, though not distinctly. When he hears it said that somebody is dead, he breaks into laughter, and keeps on laughing. This trait alone would stamp him as a Buso-child.

The Buso-Monkey

One day a man went out, carrying seventeen arrows, to hunt monkeys; but he found none. Next day he went again, and, as he walked along on the slope of the mountain called Malagu'san, he heard the sound of the chattering of monkeys in the trees. Looking up, he saw the great monkey sitting on an aluma'yag-tree. He took a shot at the monkey, but his arrow missed aim; and the next time he had no better luck. Twice eight he tried it; but he never hit the mark. The monkey seemed to lead a charmed life. Finally he took his seventeenth and last arrow, and brought down his game; the monkey fell down dead. But a voice came from the monkey's body that said, "You must carry me."

So the man picked up the monkey, and started to go back home; but on the way the monkey said, "You are to make a fire, and eat me up right here."

Then the man laid the monkey on the ground. Again came the voice,

"You will find a bamboo to put me in; by and by you shall eat me."

Off went the man to find the bamboo called laya, letting the monkey lie on the ground, where he had dropped it.

He walked on until he reached a forest of bamboo. There, swinging on a branch of the laya, was a karirik-bird. And the bird chirped to the man, "Where are you going?"

The man answered, "I am looking for bamboo to put the monkey in."

But the karirik-bird exclaimed, "Run away, quick! for by and by the monkey will become a buso. I will wait here, and be cutting the laya; then, when the monkey calls you, I will answer him."

In the mean time the monkey had become a great buso. He had only one eye, and that stood right in the middle of his forehead, looking just like the big bowl called langungan (the very bad buso have only one eye; some have only one leg).

After the Buso-monkey had waited many hours for the man to come back, he started out to look for him. When he reached the forest of laya, he called to the man, "Where are you?"

Then the karirik-bird answered from the tree, "Here I am, right here, cutting the bamboo."

But the man had run away, because the bird had sent him off, and made him run very fast.

As soon as the bird had answered the Buso, it flew off to another bamboo-tree, and there the Buso spied it, and knew that he had been fooled; and he said, "It's a man I want; you're just a bird. I don't care for you."

Directly then the Buso began to smell around the ground where the man had started to run up the mountain-side, and, as quick as he caught the scent, he trailed the man. He ran and ran, and all the time the man was running too; but soon the Buso began to gain on him. After a while, when the Buso had come close upon him, the man tried to look for some covert. He reached a big rock, and cried out, "O rock! will you give me shelter when the Buso tries to eat me?"

"No," replied the rock; "for, if I should help you, the Buso would break me off and throw me away."

Then the man ran on; and the Buso came nearer and nearer, searching behind every rock as he rushed along, and spying up into every tree, to see if, perchance, the man were concealed there.

At last the man came to the lemon-tree called kabayawa, that has long, sharp thorns on its branches. And the man cried out to the lemon-tree, "Could you protect me, if I were to hide among your leaves and flowers?"

Instantly the lemon-tree answered, "Come right up, if you want to." Then the man climbed the tree, and concealed himself in the branches, among the flowers. Very soon the Buso came under the lemon-tree, and shouted to it, "I smell a man here. You are hiding him."

The Kabayawa said, "Sure enough, here's a man! You just climb up and get him."

Then the Buso began to scramble up the tree; but as he climbed, the thorns stuck their sharp points into him. The higher he climbed, the longer and sharper grew the thorns of the tree, piercing and tearing, until they killed the Buso.

It is because the monkey sometimes turns into a Buso that many Bagobo refuse to eat monkey. But some of the mountain Bagobo eat monkey to keep off sores.

How the Moon Tricks the Buso

The Moon is a great liar. One night long ago, the Buso looked over the earth and could not discover any people, because everybody was asleep. Then Buso went to the Moon, and asked her where all the people were to be found.

"Oh, you will not find a living person on the earth!" replied the

Moon. "Everybody in the world is dead."

"Good!" thought Buso. "To-morrow I shall have a fine meal of them."

Buso never eats living flesh, only dead bodies.

Next morning, Buso started for the graveyard; but on the way he met the Sun, and stopped to speak to him.

"How about the men on earth?" he questioned.

"They're all right," said the Sun. "All the people are working and playing and cooking rice."

The Buso was furious to find himself tricked. That night he went again to the Moon and asked for the men, and, as before, the Moon assured him that everybody was dead. But the next morning the Sun showed him all the people going about their work as usual. Thus the Buso has been fooled over and over again. The Moon tells him every night the same story.

The Buso and the Cat

The cat is the best animal. She keeps us from the Buso. One night the Buso came into the house, and said to the cat, "I should like to eat your mistress."

"I will let you do it," replied the cat; "but first you must count all the hairs of my coat."

So the Buso began to count. But while he was counting, the cat kept wriggling her tail, and sticking up her back. That made her fur stand up on end, so that the Buso kept losing count, and never knew where he left off. And while the Buso was still trying to count the cat's hairs, daylight came.

This is one reason why we must not kill the cat. If a Bagobo should kill a cat, it would make him very sick. He would get skinny, and die. Some Bagobo have been known to kill the cat; but they always got sick afterwards.

How a Dog Scared the Buso

The Tigbanua' are the worst of all the Buso; they want to be eating human flesh all the time. They live in great forests,—in the pananag-tree, in the magbo-tree, in the baliti-tree, and in the liwaan-tree.

One day a man went out to hunt, and he took his dog with him. On his way to the woods, he speared a very little pig. By the time he reached the great forest, night had come. He made a little shelter, and kindled a fire. Then he cleaned the pig and cut it into pieces, and tied three sticks of wood together, and placed them on two upright pieces of wood stuck in the ground. On this paga he laid the pig-meat to broil over the flames.

By and by he got very sleepy, and thought he would go under the shelter and take a nap. But just then he heard voices up in the big trees. He listened, and heard the Tigbanua' talking to one another.

The Tigbanua' that lives in the liwaan-tree called out to the Tigbanua' that lives in the pananag-tree, "The mighty chief of all the Tigbanua', who lives in the sigmit-tree, gives this command to his people: 'Don't make fun of the man, because he has been here many times before.' "

And right there, under the trees, the man, standing by his dog, was listening to the talk of the Buso. The dog was sleeping near the fire, and he was as big as the calf of a carabao. Very quietly his master spread his own sleeping-tunic (kisi) over the dog, and crept away, leaving him asleep in the warm place. The man hid in the shelter, and waited.

Presently many of the Tigbanua' began coming down from the trees, for some of them did not give obedience (paminug) to their Datu. They gathered around the fire, and sat down. By and by, as they sat near the fire, the penis (tapo) of every one of the Tigbanua' began to grow bigger and bigger (lanag-lanag). All at once, the Tigbanua' caught sight of the tunic spread out, and showing the form of a huge head and body under it. They all thought it was the man; and they rushed up to it, and hugged it. But the dog woke up, jumped out from under the tunic, and bit the Tigbanua'. Then they all ran.

One of them climbed up the tree to his own house, the dog holding on to his leg, and biting him all the time. But when they were halfway up the tree, the dog fell down and got hurt. And the Tigbanua' called down to the dog, "Swell up, swell up!" ("Pigsa, pigsa!")

All the other Tigbanua' were afraid of the big dog, and ran away. So the man slept well all night, because the Buso could not hurt him now.

Story of Duling and the Tagamaling

Before the world was made, there were Tagamaling. The Tagamaling is the best Buso, because he does not want to hurt man all of the time. Tagamaling is actually Buso only a part of the time; that is, the month when he eats people. One month he eats human flesh, and then he is Buso; the next month he eats no human flesh, and then he is a god. So he alternates, month by month. The month he is Buso, he wants to eat man during the dark of the moon; that is, between the phases that the moon is full in the east and new in the west.

The other class of Buso, however, wants human flesh all of the time. They are the Tigbanua', the chief of whom is Datu of all the Buso. A Tigbanua' lives in his own house, and goes out only to eat the bodies of the dead.

The Tagamaling makes his house in trees that have hard wood, and low, broad-spreading branches. His house is almost like gold, and is called "Palimbing," but it is made so that you cannot see it; and, when you pass by, you think, "Oh! what a fine tree with big branches," not dreaming that it is the house of a Tagamaling. Sometimes, when you walk in the forest, you think you see one of their houses; but when you come near to the place, there is nothing. Yet you can smell the good things to eat in the house.

Once a young man named Duling, and his younger brother, went out into the woods to trap wild chickens. Duling had on his back a basket holding a decoy cock, together with the snares of running-nooses and all the parts of the trap. While they were looking for a good spot to drive in the stakes for the snare, they heard the voice of Tagamaling in the trees, saying, "Duling, Duling, come in! My mother is making a little fiesta here."

The boys looked up, and could see the house gleaming there in the branches, and there were two Tagamaling-women calling to them. In response to the call, Duling's younger brother went up quickly into the house; but Duling waited on the ground below. He wanted the Tagamaling-girls to come down to him, for he was enamoured (kalatugan) of them. Then one girl ran down to urge Duling to come up into the tree. And as soon as she came close to him, he caught her to his breast, and hugged her and caressed her.

In a moment, Duling realized that the girl was gone, and that he was holding in his arms a nanga-bush, full of thorns. He had thought to catch the girl, but, instead, sharp thorns had pricked him full of sores. Then from above he heard the woman's voice, tauntingly sweet, "Don't feel bad, Duling; for right here is your younger brother."

Yet the young man, gazing here and there, saw around him only tall trees, and could not catch a glimpse of the girl who mocked him.

Immediately, Duling, as he stood there, was turned into a rock. But the little brother married the Tagamaling-girl.

There is a place high up in the mountains of Mindanao, about eight hours' ride west of Santa Cruz, where you may see the rock, and you will know at once that it is a human figure. There is Duling, with the trap and the decoy cock on his shoulder. You may see the cock's feathers too.

The S'iring

The S'iring is the ugly man that has long nails and curly hair. He lives in the forest trees. If a boy goes into the forest without a companion, the S'iring tries to carry him off. When you meet a S'iring, he will look like your father, or mother, or some friend; and he will hide his long nails behind his back, so that you cannot see them. It is the S'iring who makes the echo (a'u'd). When you talk in a loud voice, the S'iring will answer you in a faint voice, because he wants to get you and carry you away.

There was once a boy who went without a companion into the forest, and he met a man who looked just like his own father, but it was a S'iring; and the S'iring made him believe that he was his father. The S'iring said to the boy, "Come, you must go with me. We will shoot some wild birds with our bow and arrows."

And the boy, not doubting that he heard his father's voice, followed the S'iring into the deep forest. After a while, the boy lost his memory, and forgot the way to his own house. The S'iring took him up on a high mountain, and gave him food; but the poor boy had now lost his mind, and he thought the food was a milleped one fathom long, or it seemed to him the long, slim worm called liwati.

So the days went on, the boy eating little, and growing thinner and weaker all the time. When he met any men in the forest, he grew frightened, and would run away. When he had been a long time in the forest, the S'iring called to him and said, "We will move on now."

So they started off again. When they reached the high bank of a deep and swift-flowing river, the S'iring scratched the boy with his long nails. Straightway the boy felt so tired that he could no longer stand on his legs, and then he dropped down into the ravine. He fell on the hard rocks, so that his bones were broken, and his skull split open.

All this time, the mother at home was mourning for her son, and crying all day long. But soon she arranged a little shrine (tambara) under the great tree, and, having placed there a white bowl with a few betel-nuts and some buyo-leaf as an offering for her son, she crouched on the ground and prayed for his life to the god in the sky.

Now, when the S'iring heard her prayer, he took some betel-nuts, and went to the place where the boy's body lay. On the parts where the bones were broken, he spit betel-nut, and did the same to the boy's head. Immediately the boy came to life, and felt well again. Then the S'iring took him up, and carried him to the shrine where the mother was praying; but she could not see the S'iring nor her boy. She went home crying.

That night, as the woman slept, she dreamed that a boy came close to her, and spoke about her son. "To-morrow morning," he said, "you must pick red peppers, and get a lemon, and carry them to the shrine, and burn them in the fire."

Next morning, the woman hastened to gather the peppers, and get a lemon, and with happy face she ran to the shrine under the big tree. There she made a fire, and burned the lemon and the red peppers, as the dream had told her. And, as soon as she had done this, her son appeared from under the great tree. Then his mother caught him in her arms, and held him close, and cried for joy.

When you lose your things, you may be sure that the S'iring has hidden them. What you have to do is to burn some red peppers with beeswax (tadu ka petiukan), and observe carefully the direction in which the smoke goes. The way the smoke goes points out where your things are hidden, because the S'iring is afraid of the wax of bees. He is afraid, too, of red peppers and of lemons.

How Iro Met the S'iring

Not long ago, a young man named Iro went out, about two o'clock in the afternoon, to get some tobacco from one of the neighbors. Not far from his house, he saw his friend Atun coming along; and Atun said to him, "I've got some tobacco hidden away in a place in the woods. Let us go and get it."

So they went along together. When they reached the forest, Atun disappeared, and Iro could not see which way he had gone. Then he concluded that it was not Atun, but a S'iring, whom he had met. He started for home, and reached there about eight o'clock in the evening. To his astonishment, he saw Atun sitting there in the house. Confused and wondering, he asked Atun, "Did you carry me away?"

But his friend Atun laughed, and said, "Where should I carry you? I have not been anywhere."

Then Iro was convinced that a S'iring had tried to lure him into the forest.

When you have a companion, the S'iring cannot hurt you.

Animal Stories: Metamorphosis, Explanatory Tales, Etc.

The Kingfisher and the Malaki

There came a day when the kingfisher (kobug) had nothing to drink, and was thirsty for water. Then she walked along the bed of the brook, searching for a drink; but the waters of the brook were all dried up.

Now, on that very day, the Maganud went up the mountain to get some agsam to make leglets for himself. And when he came near to where the bulla grows, he stopped to urinate, and the urine sprinkled one of the great bulla-leaves. Then he went on up the mountain. Just then, the kingfisher came along, still looking for a mountain-stream. Quickly she caught sight of the leaf of the bulla-tree all sprinkled with water; but the man had gone away. Then the kingfisher gladly drank a few drops of the water, and washed her feathers. But no sooner had she quenched her thirst, and taken a bath, than her head began to pain her. Then she went home to her little house in the ground.

Now, every day the kingfisher laid one egg, and that day she laid her egg as usual. But when the egg hatched out, it was no feathered nestling, but a baby-boy, that broke the shell.

"Oh!" cried the frightened bird. "What will become of me?" Then she ran off a little way from her nest, and started to fly away.

But the little boy cried out, "Mother, mother, don't be afraid of me!"

So the kingfisher came back to her baby. And the child grew bigger every day.

After a while, the boy was old enough to walk and play around. Then one day he went alone to the house of the Maganud, and climbed up the steps and looked in at the door. The Maganud was sitting there on the floor of his house; and the little boy ran up to him and hugged him, and cried for joy. But the Maganud was startled and dismayed; for he was a chaste malaki, and had no children. Yet this boy called him "father," and begged for ripe bananas in a very familiar manner. After they had talked for a little while, the Maganud went with the child to the home of the kingfisher.

The kingfisher had made her nest at the foot of a great hollow tree. She had dug out a hole, about four feet deep, in the soft ground, and fixed a roof by heaping over the hole the powdered rotten bark of the old tree. The roof stood up just a few inches above the ground; and when the Maganud saw it, he thought it was a mere little heap of earth. Immediately, however, as he looked at the lowly nest, it became a fine house with walls of gold, and pillars of ivory. The eaves were all hung with little bells (korung-korung); and the whole house was radiantly bright, for over it forked lighting played continually.

The kingfisher took off her feather coat, and became a lovely woman, and then she and the Malaki were married. They had bananas and cocoanut-groves, and all things, and they became rich people.

The Woman and the Squirrel

One day a woman went out to find water. She had no water to drink, because all the streams were dried up. As she went along, she saw some water in a leaf. She drank it, and washed her body. As soon as she had drunk the water, her head began to hurt. Then she went home, spread out a mat, lay down on it, and went to sleep. She slept for nine days. When she woke up, she took a comb and combed her hair. As she combed it, a squirrel-baby came out from her hair. After the baby had been in the house one week, it began to grow and jump about. It staid up under the roof of the house.

One day the Squirrel said to his mother, "O mother! I want you to go to the house of the Datu who is called 'sultan,' and take these nine kamagi and these nine finger-rings to pay for the sultan's daughter, because I want to marry her."

Then the mother went to the sultan's house and remained there an hour. The sultan said, "What do you want?"

The woman answered, "Nothing. I came for betel-nuts." Then the woman went back home.

The Squirrel met her, and said, "Where are my nine necklaces?"

"Here they are," said the woman.

But the Squirrel was angry at his mother, and bit her with his little teeth.

Again he said to his mother, "You go there and take the nine necklaces."

So the woman started off again. When she reached the sultan's house, she said to him, "I have come with these nine necklaces and these nine finger-rings that my son sends to you."

"Yes," said the sultan; "but I want my house to become gold, and I want all my plants to become gold, and everything I have to turn into gold."

But the woman left the presents to pay for the sultan's daughter. The sultan told her that he wanted his house to be turned into gold that very night. Then the woman went back and told all this to her son. The Squirrel said, "That is good, my mother."

Now, when night came, the Squirrel went to the sultan's house, and stood in the middle of the path, and called to his brother, the Mouse, "My brother, come out! I want to see you."

Then the great Mouse came out. All the hairs of his coat were of gold, and his eyes were of glass.

The Mouse said, "What do you want of me, my brother Squirrel?"

"I called you," answered the Squirrel, "for your gold coat. I want some of that to turn the sultan's house into gold."

Then the Squirrel bit the skin of the Mouse, and took off some of the gold, and left him. Then he began to turn the sultan's things into gold. First of all, he rubbed the gold on the betel-nut trees of the sultan; next, he rubbed all the other trees and all the plants; third, he rubbed the house and all the things in it. Then the sultan's town you could see as in a bright day. You would think there was no night there—always day.

All this time, the sultan was asleep. When he woke up, he was so frightened to see all his things, and his house, of gold, that he died in about two hours.

Then the Squirrel and the daughter of the sultan were married. The Squirrel staid in her father's home for one month, and then they went to live in the house of the Squirrel's mother. And they took from the sultan's place, a deer, a fish, and all kinds of food. After the sultan's daughter had lived with the Squirrel for one year, he took off his coat and became a Malaki T'oluk Waig.

The Cat

Very long ago the cocoanut used to be the head of the cat. That is why the cat loves cocoanut so much. When the Bagobo are eating cocoanut, they let the cat jump up and have some too, because her head once turned into a cocoanut. When the cat hears the Bagobo scraping cocoanut in the kitchen, she runs quickly to get some to eat.

We cut off some of the fur from the tip of the cat's tail, and put the hairs under one of the big stones (sigung) where the fire burns. This is why the cat loves the house where she lives.

When the cat dies, her gimokud takawanan goes down to Gimokudan, where the spirits of dead people go.

Why the Bagobo Likes the Cat

An old man was fishing in the brook; but the water kept getting muddy, and he did not know what was the matter. Then he went away, and he walked and walked. After he had gone some distance, he saw in the mud a big lion that eats people. The Lion had been sleeping in the mud. He said to the man, "If you'll pull me out of the mud and ride me to my town, I will give you many things." Then the man drew the Lion from the mud.

The Lion stood still a while, and then said, "Now you must ride on me."

So the man mounted the Lion, and rode until they came to a large meadow, when the Lion said, "Now I am going to eat you."

The man replied, "But first let us go and ask the Carabao."

The Lion consented, and they went on until they reached the Carabao.

"This Lion wants to eat me," complained the man.

"Yes, indeed! eat him, Lion," answered the Carabao, "for the men are all the time riding on my back, and whipping me."

There were many Carabaos in the field, and they all agreed to this.

Then the man said to the Lion, "You may eat me; but we will first go and tell the Cows."

Soon they reached the Cows' home, and the man told them that the Lion wanted to eat him.

At once the Cows exclaimed, "Yes, eat him, Lion, because all day long the people drive us away from their fields."

"All right!" assented the man; "but first let us speak to the Dogs."

When they came to the Dogs' home, the man cried, "The Lion is going to eat me."

The Dogs said to the Lion, "Devour this man; for every day, when men are eating, they beat us away from the food."

At last the man said, "Sure enough, you will eat me up, Lion; but let us just go to the Cat."

When they reached the Cat's home, they found her sitting at the door, keeping her nice house. It had groves of cocoanut-palms around it. The Cat lived all alone.

The man said to her, "This Lion wants to eat me."

"Yes, Lion," the Cat replied; "but first you make a deep hole in the ground. We will race each other into the hole. If you jump in first, then I shall lose and you will win."

And the Lion ran, and jumped into the hole. Then the Cat covered him with earth and stones until he was dead. But before he died, the Lion called to the Cat, "Whenever I see your excrement (tai), I shall eat it." That is why the Cat hides her excrement, because she is afraid the Lion will come.

Now, the Lion is the dog of the Buso.

How the Lizards got their Markings

One day the Chameleon (palas) and the Monitor-lizard (ibid) were out in a deep forest together. They thought they would try scratching each other's backs to make pretty figures on them.

First the Chameleon said to the Monitor-lizard, "You must scratch a nice pattern on my back."

So the Monitor went to work, and the Chameleon had a fine scratching. Monitor made a nice, even pattern on his back.

Then Monitor asked Chameleon for a scratching. But no sooner had Chameleon begun to work on Monitor's back than there came the sound of a dog barking. A man was hunting in the forest with his dog. The sharp barks came nearer and nearer to the two lizards; and the Chameleon got such a scare, that his fingers shook, and the pretty design he was making went all askew. Then he stopped short and ran away, leaving the Monitor with a very shabby marking on his back.

This is the reason that the monitor-lizard is not so pretty as the chameleon.

The Monkey and the Tortoise

One day, when a Tortoise was crawling slowly along by a stream, he saw a baby-monkey drinking water. Presently the Monkey ran up to the Tortoise, and said, "Let's go and find something to eat."

Not far from the stream there was a large field full of banana-trees. They looked up, and saw clusters of ripe fruit.

"That's fine!" said the Monkey, "for I'm hungry and you're hungry too. You climb first, Tortoise."

Then the Tortoise crawled slowly up the trunk; but he had got up only a little distance when the Monkey chattered these words, "Roro s'punno, roro s'punno!" ("Slide down, slide down, Tortoise!")

At once the Tortoise slipped and fell down. Then he started again to climb the tree; and again the Monkey said, "Roro s'punno!" and again the Tortoise slipped and fell down. He tried over and over again; but every time he failed, for the Monkey always said, "Roro s'punno!" and made him fall. At last he got tired and gave it up, saying to the Monkey, "Now you try it."

"It's too bad!" said the Monkey, "when we're both so hungry." Then the Monkey made just three jumps, and reached the ripe fruit. "Wait till I taste and see if they're sweet," he cried to the Tortoise, while he began to eat bananas as fast as he could.

"Give me some," begged the Tortoise.

"All right!" shouted the Monkey; "but I forgot to notice whether it was sweet." And he kept on eating, until more than half of the fruit was gone.

"Drop down just one to me!" pleaded the Tortoise.

"Yes, in a minute," mumbled the Monkey.

At last, when but three bananas were left on the tree, the Monkey called, "Look up! shut your eyes" (Langag-ka! pudung-nu yan matanu).

The Tortoise did so. The Monkey then told him to open his mouth, and he obeyed. Then the Monkey said, "I'll peel this one piece of banana for you" (Luitan-ko 'ni sebad abok saging).

Now, the Monkey was sitting on a banana-leaf, directly over the Tortoise; but, instead of banana, he dropped his excrement into the Tortoise's mouth. The Tortoise screamed with rage; but the Monkey jumped up and down, laughing at him. Then he went on eating the remainder of the bananas.

The Tortoise then set himself to work at making a little hut of bamboo-posts, with a roof and walls of leaves. The upper ends of the bamboo he sharpened, and let them project through the roof; but the sharp points were concealed by the leaves. It was like a trap for pigs (sankil).

When the Monkey came down from the banana-tree, the Tortoise said, "You climb this other tall tree, and look around at the sky. If the sky is dark, you must call to me; for the rain will soon come. Then you jump down on the roof of our little house here. Never mind if it breaks in, for we can soon build a stronger one."

The Monkey accordingly climbed the tree, and looked at the sky. "It is all very dark!" he exclaimed. "Jump quick, then!" cried the Tortoise.

So the Monkey jumped; but he got killed from the sharp bamboo-points on which he landed.

Then the Tortoise made a fire, and roasted the Monkey. He cut off the Monkey's ears, and they turned into buyo-leaves. He cut out the heart, and it turned into betel-nut. He took out the brain, and it became lime (apog). He made the tail into pungaman. The stomach he made into a basket. He put into the basket the betel and the lime and the pungaman and the buyo, and crawled away.

Soon he heard the noise of many animals gathered together. He found the monkeys and the deer and the pigs and the wild birds having a big rice-planting. All the animals were rejoiced to see the Tortoise coming with a basket, for they all wanted to chew betel. The monkeys ran up, chattering, and tried to snatch the betel-nuts; but the Tortoise held them back, saying, "Wait a minute! By and by I will give you some."

Then the monkeys sat around, waiting, while the Tortoise prepared the betel-nut. He cut the nuts and the pungaman into many small pieces, and the buyo-leaf too, and gave them to the monkeys and the other animals. Everybody began to chew; and the Tortoise went away to a distance about the length of one field (sebad kinamat), where he could get out of sight, under shelter of some trees. Then he called to the monkeys, "All of you are eating monkey, just like your own body: you are chewing up one of your own family."

At that, all the monkeys were angry, and ran screaming to catch the Tortoise. But the Tortoise had hid under the felled trunk of an old palma brava tree. As each monkey passed close by the trunk where the Tortoise lay concealed, the Tortoise said, "Drag your membrum! here's a felled tree" (Supa tapo! basio').

Thus every monkey passed by clear of the trunk, until the last one came by; and he was both blind and deaf. When he followed the rest, he could not hear the Tortoise call out, "Supa tapo! basio';" and his membrum struck against the fallen trunk. He stopped, and became aware of the Tortoise underneath. Then he screamed to the rest; and all the monkeys came running back, and surrounded the Tortoise, threatening him.

"What do you want?" inquired the Tortoise.

"You shall die," cried the monkeys. "Tell us what will kill you. We will chop you to pieces with the axe."

"Oh, no! that won't hurt me in the least," replied the Tortoise. "You can see the marks on my shell, where my father used to cut my body: but that didn't kill me."

"We will put you in the fire, then, and burn you to death," chorussed the monkeys. "Will that do?"

"Fire does not hurt me," returned the Tortoise. "Look at my body! See how brown it is where my father used to stick me into the fire."

"What, then, is best to kill you?" urged the monkeys.

"The way to kill me," replied the Tortoise, "is to take the punch used for brass, bulit, and run it into my rectum. Then throw me into the big pond, and drown me."

Then the monkeys did as they were told, and threw him into the pond. But the Tortoise began to swim about in the water.

Exultantly he called to the monkeys, "This is my own home: you see I don't drown." And the lake was so deep that the monkeys could not get him.

Then the monkeys hurried to and fro, summoning all the animals in the world to drink the water in the lake. They all came,—deer, pigs, jungle-fowl, monkeys, and all the rest,—and began to drink. They covered their pagindis with leaves, so that the water could not run out of their bodies. After a time, they had drunk so much that the lake became shallow, and one could see the Tortoise's back.

But the red-billed bakaka-bird that lived in a tree by the water was watching; and as quick as the back of the Tortoise came into sight, the bird flew down and picked off the leaves from the pagindis of the deer. Then the water ran out from their bodies until the lake rose again, and covered the Tortoise. Satisfied, the bird flew back into the tree. But the deer got fresh leaves to cover their pagindis, and began to drink again. Then the bird flew to the monkeys, and began to take the leaves from their pagindis; but one monkey saw him doing it, and slapped him. This made the bird fall down, and then all the monkeys left the Tortoise in the lake, and ran to revenge themselves on the bird.

They snatched him up, pulled out every one of his feathers with their fingers, and laid him naked upon the stump of a tree. All the animals went home, leaving the bird on the stump.

Two days later, one Monkey came to look at the Bakaka. Little feathers were beginning to grow out; but the Monkey thought the bird was dead.

"Maggots are breeding in it," said the Monkey.

Three more days passed, and then the Monkey came again. The Bakaka's feathers had grown out long by that time; and the Monkey said, "It was all rotten, and the pigs ate it."

But the bird had flown away. He flew to the north until he reached a meadow with a big tual-tree in the middle. The tree was loaded with ripe fruit. Perched on one of the branches, the bird ate all he wanted, and when done he took six of the fruit of the tual, and made a necklace for himself. With this hung round his neck, he flew to the house where the old Monkey lived, and sat on the roof. He dropped one tual through the roof, and it fell down on the floor, where all the little monkey-children ran for it, dancing and screaming.

"Don't make such a noise!" chided the old Monkey, "and do not take the tual, for the Bakaka will be angry, and he is a great bird."

But the bird flew down into the house, and gave one tual to the old Monkey.

"That is good," said the old Monkey, tasting it. "Tell me where you got it." But the bird would not tell. Then the old monkey stood up, and kissed him, and begged to be taken to the tual-tree.

At last the Bakaka said to all the monkeys, "Three days from now you may all go to the tual-tree. I want you all to go, the blind monkey too. Go to the meadow where the grass grows high, and there, in the centre of the meadow, is the tual-tree. If you see the sky and the air black, do not speak a word; for if you speak, you will get sick."

At the set time, all the monkeys started for the meadow, except one female monkey that was expecting a baby. The deer and all the other animals went along, except a few of the females who could not go. They all reached the meadow-grass; and the monkeys climbed up the tual-tree that stood in the centre of the field, until all the branches were full of monkeys. The birds and the jungle-fowl flew up in the tree; but the deer and the other animals waited clown on the ground.

Then the sky grew black, for the Bakaka and the Tortoise were going around the meadow with lighted sticks of balekayo, and setting fire to the grass. The air was full of smoke, and the little monkeys were crying; but the old Monkey bit them, and said, "Keep still, for the Bakaka told us not to speak."

But the meadow-grass was all ablaze, and the flames crept nearer and nearer to the tual-tree. Then all the monkeys saw the fire, and cried, "Oh! what will become of us?"

Some of the birds and most of the chickens flew away; but some died in the flames. A few of the pigs ran away, but most of them died. The other animals were burned to death. Not a single monkey escaped, save only the female monkey who staid at home. When her baby was born, it was a boy-monkey. The mother made it her husband, and from this pair came many monkeys.

It was the same with the deer. All were burned, except one doe who staid at home. When her little fawn was born, it was a male. She made it her husband, and from this one pair came many deer.

The Crow and the Golden Trees

The liver of the crow is "medicine" for many pains and for sickness. On this account the Bagobo kills the crow so that he may get his liver for "medicine." The liver is good to eat, either cooked or raw. If you see a crow dead, you can get its liver and eat some of it, and it will be "medicine" for your body.

The crow never makes its nest in low-growing trees, but only in tall, big trees. Far from here, the old men say, in the land where the sun rises, there are no more living trees; for the scorching heat of the sun has killed them.all, and dried up the leaves. There they stand, with naked branches, all bare of leaves. Only two trees there have not died from the heat. The trunks of these trees are of gold, and all their leaves of silver. But if any bird lights on one of these trees, it falls down dead. The ground under the two trees is covered with the bones of little birds and big birds that have died from perching on the trees with the golden trunks and the silver leaves. These two trees are full of a resin that makes all the birds die. Only the crow can sit on the branches, and not die. Hence the crow alone, of all the birds, remains alive in the land of the sunrise.

No man can get the resin from these trees. But very long ago, in the days of the Mona, there came a Malaki T'oluk Waig to the trees. He had a war-shield that shone brightly, for it had a flame of fire always burning in it. And this Malaki came to the golden trees and took the precious resin from their trunks.

An Ata Story

Alelu'k and Alebu'tud

Alelu'k and Alebu'tud lived together in their own house. They had no neighbors. One day Alelu'k said to his wife, "I must go and hunt some pigs."

Then he started out to hunt, taking with him his three dogs. He did not find any wild pigs; but before long he sighted a big deer with many-branched antlers. The dogs gave chase and seized the deer, and held it until the man came up and killed it with the sharp iron spike that tipped his long staff (tidalan). Then the man tied to the deer's antlers a strong piece of rattan, and dragged it home.

When he reached his house, his wife met him joyfully; and they were both very happy, because they had now plenty of meat. They brought wood and kindled a fire, and fixed over the fire a frame of wood tied to upright posts stuck into the ground. On the frame they laid the body of the deer to singe off the hair over the flames. And when the hair was all burned off, and the skin clean, Alelu'k began to cut off pieces of venison, and Alebu'tud got ready the big clay pot, and poured into it water to boil the meat. But there was only a little water in the house, so Alubu'tud took her bucket (sekkadu), and hurried down to the river. When she reached there, she stood with her bare feet in the stream, and dipped the bucket into the stream, and took it out full of water. But, just as she turned to climb up the river-bank, an enormous fish jumped out of the river, seized her, dragged her down, and devoured her.

At home, Alelu'k was watching for his wife to come back bringing the water. Day after day he waited for her, and all day long he was crying from sorrow.

The man (Alelu'k) symbolizes a big black ant that makes its nest in a hollow tree. The woman (Alebu'tud) is a little worm that lives in the palma brava tree. The fish is another man who carried off Alelu'k's wife.

Made in the USA
Lexington, KY
14 December 2015